An Amazing Discovery!

Professor Bullfinch pointed the nozzle of his invention, the C-ray, at the wall of the cave. Then he sat next to his friend and showed him how to operate it. Dr. Tresselt sat absorbed, moving first one knob, then the other. On the screen, a strange shape grew. It looked like a fan, with a large hole below it like an eye, then a curved eagle's beak, and two spiky horns jutting forward.

"Congratulations!" Dr. Tresselt said, in a voice that trembled with excitement. "Your C-ray is more than a success. Look at that! Doesn't it look familiar?"

The Professor stared. Then, almost in a whisper, he said, "It does indeed. A fossil skull. The skull of a dinosaur!"

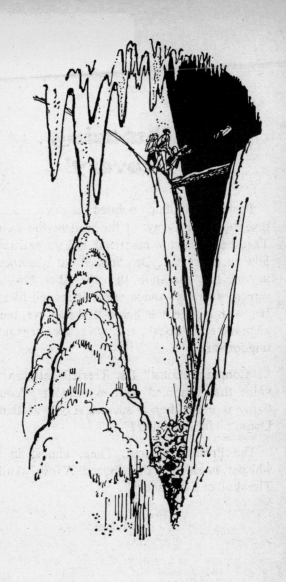

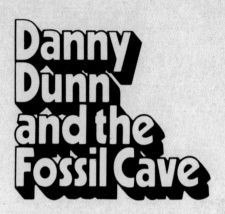

Danny Dunn and the Fossil Cave

Jay Williams and
Raymond Abrashkin

Illustrated by Brinton Turkle

AN ARCHWAY PAPERBACK
POCKET BOOKS · NEW YORK

**POCKET BOOKS, a Simon & Schuster division of
GULF & WESTERN CORPORATION**
1230 Avenue of the Americas, New York, N.Y. 10020

ISBN: 0-671-43290-7

First Pocket Books printing August, 1979

10 9 8 7 6 5 4 3

AN ARCHWAY PAPERBACK and ARCH are trademarks
of Simon & Schuster.

Printed in the U.S.A.

IL 4+

*This book is for Sally Hyman
and for Lance Richard King.*

ACKNOWLEDGMENTS

The authors wish to express their thanks to John Atwood—Director of Research, Perkin-Elmer Corporation—for technical advice and information, and to Rose Wyler of Science Materials Center, for information concerning the Geiger-Müller Counter.

Contents

1
From a Clear Sky

Danny Dunn, his face flaming almost as red as his hair from the August heat, came panting up on the summit of the Sugarloaf, the highest point of the hills above the town of Midston. He paused, mopping his forehead, and looked out over the wide valley below, at the little toy blocks of houses, the red brick of the College buildings, and beyond them, the shining silver of the reservoir lake.

Then he shouted over his shoulder, "Irene! Joe! Come on! It's this way."

Irene Miller and Joe Pearson toiled up behind him. Joe's long thin face was even gloomier than usual, and as he came to the flat stones at the summit he gave a loud, sad sneeze.

"Bless you," said Irene, switching her

1

glossy dark pony-tail from side to side to drive away the gnats which buzzed around her face. "Don't tell me you're catching cold on a hot day like this?"

"Id's nod a code," Joe mumbled. "Id's addergy."

"Addergy? Goodness, Dan, do you think that's something catching?" Irene grinned.

"Allergy, I guess he means," Danny said. "Poor old Joe. He's allergic to climbing, to exercise, to perspiring, to mountains—"

"Okay, okay," Joe howled, flapping his hands. "Very fuddy. The side of the hill is all cubbered wid godded-rod, ad I'b addergic to *dat!*"

Danny looked sympathetically at his friend's red nose and streaming eyes. "Well, there's no goldenrod up here," he said. "And the breeze ought to make you feel better. Let's rest for a minute."

They made themselves comfortable on the sun-warmed stone, and Danny pointed to a bulge of gray rock swelling out on the mountain face below them. A wide crack split it diagonally.

"We can follow that crack down," he said.

Joe glanced at his watch. "Eleved o'clock," he said.

"I know just what you're thinking," said

Danny. "Do we have time to find the cave, explore it, and still get home in time for lunch? Right?"

Joe nodded, and blew his nose several times. He was beginning to feel a good deal better in spite of himself, and when he spoke again it was in a clearer voice. "It isn't that I'm hungry," he said. "It's just that I haven't had anything to eat since breakfast."

"Not counting those two candy bars and the apple," said Irene.

"I mean *real* food."

Dan, with his elbows on his knees, peered out over the countryside. "Gosh, it's pretty up here," he said. "Makes you feel like a giant. Just think, there was a time when all that valley was water."

"Water? You mean some kind of flood?" said Joe.

"No, Professor Bullfinch says that all this part of the country was once covered by a sea. What we're standing on was part of the bottom."

"Good thing it isn't a sea now," Joe remarked. "We'd have to go to school wearing aqualungs."

"Oh, Joe, that was millions of years ago," said Irene. "Maybe even before the dinosaurs lived."

3

"Then how does Professor Bullfinch know about it? He's no dinosaur," said Joe. He lay back and stared up at the sky, yawning.

"Scientists find out from studying the rocks and the clay and sand, and types of earth, and the fossils in them," Danny replied. "And believe me, what Professor Bullfinch doesn't know about science isn't worth knowing."

Danny had been brought up in the house of Professor Euclid Bullfinch, who taught at Midston College and who was famous for his private researches. Dan's father had died when the boy was very young, and Mrs. Dunn had taken the job of housekeeper for the Professor. Between the scientist and the child a real affection had grown up, almost like that of father and son, and the Professor had taught Dan a great deal about the wonders of science.

The boy continued, "They've found fossils of shellfish and plants and things that show how the sea bottom filled up with mud. Then something—maybe earthquakes—changed the course of the streams and the sea dried up or receded. Now there are only a few little trickles left, and Midston River, and the reservoir."

"Gosh, maybe we'll find some fossils in the cave," murmured Irene.

"If we ever reach it," said Joe. "Come on,

let's get going. The sooner we find it, the sooner we can go find some sandwiches.''

Danny began the descent along the crack in the rock, setting his feet in it with care and bracing his hands against the face of the stone. After a short distance, the crack widened until it was a narrow shelf that ran diagonally along the rocky face. This, in turn, gave way to great ragged boulders among which grew scrub oaks and junipers. There were blueberry bushes, too, weedy grass, and then, a little further down, the woods began.

Dan led his friends between the dark trunks of the pines. The ground was slippery with needles, and there was a spicy smell of resin in their nostrils. Gray beech trees and the rough bark of maples appeared, and the going became harder as the smooth carpet of needles gave way to underbrush, to partridge berry and sassafras, and tangles of blackberry vines. A pheasant shot up like a rocket with a clap of wings that made all three young people jump. A jay scolded them noisily as they clattered down the slope hanging on to saplings to keep from sliding headlong. The forest thinned. They emerged beside a long ridge of rock, partly covered with moss and shrubs, that stuck out of the ground like the back of a giant beast.

"It's not far from here," said Danny, with satisfaction.

Joe groaned. "Not far! That's what you've been saying ever since you talked us into coming with you this morning. If you had told me I was going to have to climb up over Sugarloaf—!"

"Yes, Dan," said Irene. "Why couldn't we have come right up this side, nearest the town? It would have been shorter."

Danny nodded. "I know. But the trouble is, when I first found the cave, last spring, I didn't mark the trail to it. I was looking for mineral specimens for my collection and I took the road from the end of town up behind Sugarloaf, and past Rose Hill. Then I climbed Sugarloaf and started down this side. So I remember the landmarks from this direction but not the other."

He made his way down the slope until he was standing in the shadow of the ridge. When his friends had joined him, he said, "Now, let's see. I followed the bottom of the ridge and came out on a kind of point of ground where there was a big white oak. The cave was just below it . . . I think."

"You *think?*" Joe said.

"No, I'm sure of it. Stop worrying, Joe."

He strode resolutely on. But suddenly, Irene caught his sleeve.

"Listen," she said. "What was that?"

They stood still, cocking their heads. "I don't hear anything," said Danny.

"There it is again. Sh!"

They all heard it now, a faint, sharp tapping as of metal striking stone. It seemed to come from the ridge at their backs.

"That's just a woodpecker," Danny said, shrugging.

"Doesn't sound like a woodpecker to me," said Joe. "More like a pebble-pecker. Tell you what—let's go home."

Danny frowned at his friend. "You don't really mean that, Joe."

"I don't? Oh. I thought I did."

"And anyway, I'm not going to turn back now," Dan went on. "When I found the cave, I didn't have any light with me, not even a match. I planned to come back next day, but the next day was a school day and I forgot. Then, next time I remembered about it there was a baseball game I had to play in. Something always interfered—that camping trip one week end, and then Irene's birthday, and—gosh, all sorts of things. I wouldn't have thought of it today, except that Professor Bullfinch said something about his old friend, the geologist, coming to visit us. Now that we're here, nothing's going to stop me."

Joe sighed. "Oh, I know. But trouble can come to you out of a clear blue sky, Danny. Like that time you promised Miss Arnold you'd never meddle with the science experiments in class again. Then, you dropped a little sulphur in that test tube when she wasn't looking. Phew! It took days to get the smell out of the classroom."

"I just wanted to see what would happen," Danny said, indignantly. "But anyway, that's got nothing to do with today. This time, we've got flashlights, there won't be any trouble, and nothing's going to happen."

He turned away. Before he could take another step, something rang against the stones above his head, shot out into the air, and landed with a thump in the grass at his feet as if it had dropped from the sky.

2
Danny's Choice

For a long moment, the young people stood motionless, staring. Then Danny stooped to pick up the thing.

"Don't touch it!" Irene gasped.

"Why not?" said Danny. "It's only an old hammer, after all."

He turned it over, examining it curiously.

Joe tilted his head back. "What'd I tell you?" he said. "I didn't hear any plane. That thing must have fallen from a flying saucer. Are you sure it's just a hammer? Maybe it's a death ray shaped like a hammer."

"I'm almost sure it isn't," said a strange voice.

Looking upward in astonishment, the three

"I'm a geologist."

saw a short, weatherbeaten man regarding them from the top of the ridge. He was dressed in a corduroy jacket patched with leather on the elbows, but there was nothing ragged or dirty about him. He had the look of one who had traveled far, an outdoorsman, or an explorer. His hair was white above his sunburned face, but his eyes were bright blue, sharp, and lively.

"I'm terribly sorry," he said. "I hope nobody was hurt."

"We're all right," Danny answered.

The stranger climbed quickly down the ridge. "I had just chipped out a fine little cephalopod, and I laid my hammer on the rock above me. It slid down."

He held out a lump of stone and the young people could see that it had a faint marking on it, or rather, *in* it: a small, coiled shape like a snail-shell.

"That's what I found," said the man.

"That's a sifflepod?" said Joe. "It looks like a snail."

"The cephalopods were molluscs, something like—well—sea snails," the other said.

"Oh, then you're a fossil hunter?" asked Irene.

"Not exactly. I'm a geologist. But I can't resist a nice specimen."

"I knew you were a geologist," said Danny.

"I could tell by the shape of your hammer. Are you working at Midston College?"

"Oh, dear no," said the other, with a smile. "I'm just visiting here. Although heaven knows what Bullfinch must think. I knew I ought to phone him, but when I got off that early train and looked up at these hills, I thought to myself, 'What beautiful examples of sedimentary rock!' I got out my hammer, left my suitcase in the waiting room, and—well, here I am."

At the mention of Professor Bullfinch's name, Danny snapped his fingers. "Now I know who you are," he exclaimed. "You're Doctor Tresselt, and you're coming to stay with us."

"I am undoubtedly Dr. Tresselt," said the geologist. "But I think you're mistaken. I'm going to stay with Professor Bullfinch. Not that I wouldn't like to stay with you," he added, in a kindly tone. "I'm very fond of children. I have three or four of my own."

"I know," Danny said.

"You do? I didn't think my children had any friends in this neighborhood."

"No, I mean I know you're going to stay with Professor Bullfinch. I live with him. I'm Danny Dunn. My mother is his housekeeper."

"Well, I'm delighted to meet you," said Dr. Tresselt, shaking the boy's hand warmly.

"And these are your brother and sister, no doubt?"

Irene giggled. "My name's Irene Miller, Dr. Tresselt. I live next door to Dan."

"Her father teaches astronomy at Midston," Danny added. "And this is my friend, Joe Pearson."

"Nice to know you both," Dr. Tresselt said. "Now, if you'll excuse me, I think I'll return to the ledge. There are some very attractive fossils—"

"Jumping catfish!" said Danny. "Wait a minute, sir. I—I really think you ought to start for town. If you got in on the early train, Professor Bullfinch will be worrying about you. It's past eleven o'clock."

"Hmm. Yes, I suppose you're right." Dr. Tresselt shaded his eyes with his hand and looked about. "Unfortunately, I haven't the faintest idea how to get back to town. But never mind. Bullfinch will certainly find *me*. He was always very good at that sort of thing when we were in school together. Goodbye."

And with that, he turned away.

"Dr. Tresselt!" cried Danny. "Gee, excuse me, but—well, *we* know the way to town."

"Of course you do," the geologist beamed. "An excellent idea. You run along and tell Bullfinch where I am. He'll understand."

He waved his hand at them and started to climb the ridge.

"What'll we do?" Irene whispered. "Just leave him?"

"We can't," said Danny. "It wouldn't be fair to the Professor. Anyway—he forgot his hammer."

At that moment, Dr. Tresselt returned. "My hammer," he said, apologetically. "Thanks very much."

"Listen, Dr. Tresselt," Danny said, desperately, "I know my mother's expecting you for lunch. She'll be very disappointed. And I know the Professor's looking forward to seeing you. I really think you ought to come along with us. Then you can come back up here this afternoon, or tomorrow. After all, you are supposed to stay for a week."

"Yes, that's true." Dr. Tresselt tapped the hammer against his palm. "I mustn't be so selfish. . . . The fact is, you see, I'm afraid I sometimes let my interest in my work get the better of me. You're quite right, of course."

He straightened, decisively. "You're a very good conscience, Danny. I ought to hire you. Let's go, then."

They started off together, directly down the hill, knowing that sooner or later they'd come out in the meadows above the town. But they had only gone a short distance when Joe, pointing ahead, said, "Hey, look, Dan! That big white oak on the point of rock. Isn't that the one—?"

Danny glanced at it. There, sure enough, was the tree which marked the site of the cave. He looked at his friends, and then back at Dr. Tresselt, strolling behind them and whistling happily. He heaved a deep sigh. He knew perfectly well that if the geologist saw the cave, he would go no further.

Then he did one of the bravest things he had ever done. "It's just an old tree," he said. "Come on, let's get Dr. Tresselt home."

3
Channel 25

They went, first, to the railroad station to pick up Dr. Tresselt's suitcase, and then took a taxi home. Professor Bullfinch came out to meet the cab and greeted his old friend enthusiastically.

"My dear Alvin," he said. "Glad to see you. Up to your old tricks, eh?"

"I couldn't resist the hills, Euclid," said Dr. Tresselt. "Some beautiful limestone! If these youngsters hadn't dragged me away, I'd still be there."

Professor Bullfinch took off his glasses and wiped them, chuckling. "I'm grateful to you, all three," he said.

"But weren't you worried?" asked Irene.

"The train came in at nine o'clock. We thought you'd have the police out looking for Dr. Tresselt."

"Oh, Dr. Tresselt always manages to find his way back somehow," the Professor said. "He was lost in the Navajo desert for three weeks, once, but he found himself all right in the end, and brought back a very important report on rock formations, as well."

"I've heard about absent-minded professors. . . ," Joe whispered to Danny.

The Professor overheard him. "Not absent-minded, Joe," he said. "People say that of scientists because they don't understand how fascinating our work can be. It can absorb your attention so that you forget everything else. Dr. Tresselt is far from absent-minded in everyday affairs—I've never known him to wind up the cat and put the clock out, for instance—but when he is at work on a project, he tends to forget the rest of the world."

Joe blushed. "I'm sorry," he said. "I guess I know what you mean. It's the way I am when I'm working on a poem, for instance."

"Exactly," said Dr. Tresselt. "In fact, scientists and artists are alike in many ways."

They all went into the house, and Mrs. Dunn, a comfortable, jolly-looking woman with hair as red as her son's, shook Dr. Tresselt's hand.

"Professor Bullfinch told me we might not see you until dinner-time," she said. "Fortunately, I didn't believe him. Lunch will be ready in a few minutes. Come along, Dr. Tresselt, and I'll show you to your room."

The three grownups went upstairs. Danny sighed, jamming his hands deep into his pockets.

"Well, I'm glad we got him home," he said. "But I sure hated to leave that cave."

"What?" said Joe. "You mean that the tree I saw really was the one that marked where the entrance was?"

"I knew that," Irene said, quietly. "And Danny, I think it was—well—noble of you."

Danny shrugged, kicking at the rug with one toe. "Yeah, I must have been sick or something. I'll just never find the way back to that spot."

"Yes, you will," Irene smiled mischievously. "I dropped back, you know, and when I did I spotted the cave entrance. So, as we went down the hill, I marked the trail by breaking twigs so that they pointed back toward it, and by tying knots in the long grass. We can find the way easily."

Danny brightened. "Gosh, Irene, you're

great! I was so busy with Dr. Tresselt that I never even thought of doing that.''

''He's nice, isn't he?'' Irene said.

''There's one thing,'' said Joe. ''How could you tell that was a geologist's hammer? I didn't know geologists went around hammering things.'' He scratched his head. ''To tell the truth, I don't know what they *do* go around doing.''

''Geologists study the earth,'' Danny replied. ''They study the rocks, and how mountains were formed, and how old the earth is, and what happens to rivers and lakes and oceans. They have to know all sorts of sciences—botany, chemistry, physics, mineralogy. They have these special hammers, with narrow heads and sharp picks on them, so they can take samples of rocks and minerals.''

He turned down the long hall that led to Professor Bullfinch's private laboratory, which was built on to the back of the house. ''Let's go look in the Professor's library,'' he said. ''I want to see what Dr. Tresselt meant when he talked about 'sedimentary rock.' ''

''I'll join you later,'' Joe said. ''I've—um—got dirt all over my hands. I'll just run into the kitchen and wash up.''

He left them, and Dan and Irene went on to

the laboratory, Irene remarking, "Joe must have sunstroke or something. That's the first time I've ever heard him say right out that he *wanted* to wash his hands."

The laboratory consisted of two rooms, one small one fitted with shelves on which were books, notebooks, and files, and a larger one in which were stone-topped tables, stools, and all the varied equipment the Professor needed for his researches.

"Hey, look!" Danny said, as they entered this large room. "Professor Bullfinch has a portable TV set."

On one of the lab tables stood a small metal case with a glass screen on one side about a foot square, and a blunt, cone-shaped projection on the other.

"I didn't know the Professor watched television programs," said Irene.

"Oh, he must be using this for experiments," Danny said. "Hmm . . . I wonder if it's one of those color sets."

He examined the top of the case, in which were set tuning dials and switches, like those in an ordinary television set. "This dial must show the channels," he said. "But gosh! this *must* be an experimental model of some kind, because it goes up to Channel 75."

He studied the switches for a moment and then snapped one of them. The set began to hum softly, and the screen glowed.

"Let's try Channel 25," he said. "Maybe it comes from some foreign country."

He twiddled the knobs until a picture suddenly came into focus. He and Irene stared at it.

It was obviously a kitchen, although everything was shadowy and indistinct, and no details showed. They could make out a sink, a window, and part of a table. It looked very much like a shadowgraph, in which only the silhouettes of things showed against the light.

"It's not very clear, is it?" Irene said. "And it's certainly not in color."

"I'll see if I can get it a little sharper," said Danny. He turned one of the dials.

"Look!" Irene cried. "The picture's moving."

As the dial turned, the scene itself moved, as though the invisible camera were traveling. All at once something else came into view.

It was unmistakably a refrigerator. The door stood open. A figure straightened up, holding something which they decided was the leg of a chicken. The figure did a little jig and then began to gnaw at the chicken leg.

"You know," said Dan, "there's something awfully familiar about that television actor, even though all you can see is his outline."

Irene put her hands over her mouth to stifle a scream of laughter.

"The hair—the long nose—the way he moves," she said. "Of course he looks familiar. It's Joe!"

4
The See-Ray

Danny rubbed his nose thoughtfully, as he gazed at the image on the screen. "I think you're right," he said, slowly. "And you know something else? I don't think this is a television set."

"That is correct, my boy," said the Professor, from behind him.

He had come into the laboratory that instant, with Dr. Tresselt, and he walked over and put a friendly hand on Danny's shoulder.

"Gosh, Professor, I didn't mean to fool with it," Danny said. "But it does look just like a portable television set, and I thought—"

"No harm done," said Professor Bullfinch. "I can understand your confusion. As a matter of fact, I was just about to demonstrate it to

Dr. Tresselt, so you've saved me the trouble of turning it on."

He beckoned to the geologist to come closer. "Look here, Alvin. It is set for a distance of twenty-five feet."

"Oh," said Danny. "Not Channel 25."

"No." The Professor laughed. "So far, this experimental model has a range of about seventy-five feet. What you are seeing now is— um—the kitchen on the other side of that wall."

Dr. Tresselt stooped to peer into the screen. "Very interesting," he said. "So this is the C-ray."

"A little joke of my own," smiled the Professor. *"See*-ray."

"A kind of X-ray, actually?"

"Well, a radiation operating at the same short wave length as X-ray. But I produce it so that a much smaller amount is easily detectable. I can thus time the reflection of the rays almost like—well—radar. As you see, the screen is similar to that of a radarscope. But the sensitivity is so great that I can detect it easily, and thus there is no radiation danger."

"I see," said Dr. Tresselt. "The same job with less juice, you might say."

"Exactly. I thought it might have some value in geology, or mineralogy, since you can, in effect, see right through solid rock with it.''

The geologist shook his head. "We'd have to try it. It might develop all sorts of bugs under field conditions. And I doubt that it would be able to select between layers of, say, limestone and sandstone."

"That's why I wanted to show it to you," said the Professor. "I thought you might take it with you on your next expedition."

Dr. Tresselt was looking at the screen again.

"Whatever else it does, it certainly shows up icebox raiders very well," he said. "I presume that's your friend Joe?"

"Yes, it is," Danny said. "And—well, don't you think, Professor, that if the machine can pick out Joe and what he's eating as well as it does, that it could show fossils, or crystals, in rocks?"

The Professor stroked his chin. "Not quite the same, Dan," he replied. "In this case, the ray is probing through a solid wall to pick up objects in empty space—the kitchen. But Dr. Tresselt isn't sure it will be able to select objects buried in another solid, like stone."

"It was good thinking, though," said Dr. Tresselt. "You certainly are interested in science, Dan. How about you, Irene? Don't you sometimes feel left out of things?"

Irene looked indignant. Before she could answer, Danny said, "Gosh, no. She knows more than I do about some branches of science. Not very much, though," he added, hastily.

"I'm going to be a physicist when I go to college," Irene said. "You know there *are* women who are scientists—"

Dr. Tresselt lifted his hands apologetically. "I'm sorry," he said. "You're right. I spoke without thinking."

Irene looked happier.

"She's so crazy about science, she even wears it," Danny grinned.

"I'm afraid I don't understand," said the geologist, looking perplexed. "How can you *wear* science?"

Professor Bullfinch snapped off his C-ray machine, with a chuckle.

"I think I know what Danny means. Irene has been making up a science charm bracelet. Aren't you wearing it today, my dear?"

"No, Professor, I forgot it," said Irene.

"All the charms on it stand for different branches of science," Danny explained. "She's got a four-leaf clover that stands for botany, and a lump if iron—one of the elements—for chemistry. What else is there, Irene?"

Irene frowned. "Well, there's a tiny magnifying glass for microscopy, and a computer switch for mathematics, and a little nut and bolt for engineering, and a dried cocoon for insect studies, and on my birthday my father gave me a tiny gold tag with Einstein's equation—$E = MC^2$—engraved on it. That's for physics.''

"What a list," laughed Dr. Tresselt. "Excellent! Sounds very complete. But what have you for geology?"

"Gee, I haven't anything yet. What do you suggest?"

"We must try to find her a little fossil, or perhaps a handsome little crystal of some sort, eh, Bullfinch?"

The Professor nodded. Before he could reply, however, Joe came into the laboratory. "Hello, everybody," he said. "I just came in to say goodbye. I've got to go home for lunch."

Danny looked innocently at his friend. "Hands all washed?" he asked.

"Sure. Why?"

"But Joe—you don't mean to say you still have room for lunch?" Irene cried.

"Why not?" Joe said, but his face began to turn red.

Danny put his fingers to his forehead. "I am in contact with the spirit world," he said, in a mysterious voice. "I am now receiving a message from beyond—from a ghost—from the ghost of a roast chicken. It tells me you went into the refrigerator while my mother was out of the kitchen, and that you took a drumstick and ate it. . . ."

Joe gave a long whistle. Then he shrugged.

"Okay," he said. "I confess. What did you do, peek through the window?"

"Easier than that," said Danny. "We watched you through the wall."

"Uh-huh," Joe grunted. "Why didn't you walk right through, then, and show me where the mayonnaise was?"

"It's true, Joe," said Irene. "Ask the Professor. We watched you with his new C-ray."

"Nobody's safe any more," Joe mumbled. "I always got into trouble with Danny. Now, I can't even trust the Professor. Next thing you know, there'll be rays to make sure you do your homework, and rays that make you wash behind the ears—"

"Come, now, Joe," said Professor Bullfinch, taking out his pipe and filling it. "Things aren't quite that bad."

"Not yet, maybe," Joe said, gloomily. "I should think you scientists could find something better to invent than a ray for spying on a poor hungry kid like me . . . pale, and thin . . . just picking up a few crumbs. . . ."

The others burst into laughter. The Professor said, "Joe, I give you my word I didn't invent the C-ray to make you unhappy. We'll never use it to watch you again."

"That cheers me up," said Joe, looking sadder than ever.

"I hate to break up the National Research Council convention," said Mrs. Dunn, putting her head into the room, "but lunch is ready."

Danny said, "Oh, Mom. Do you think Joe and Irene—"

"I've already called their mothers," Mrs. Dunn said, placidly. "There's enough lunch for everyone. Joe won't need quite as much as the rest, as he's already had part of his."

"Oh, help!" wailed Joe. "How about that? She's got a C-ray, too!"

Irene sniffed. "Hmf! You ought to know that mothers don't need science to find out things. You probably left the drumstick on the table."

"On a chair, as a matter of fact," said Mrs. Dunn. "And his face is greasy. Come on, everyone."

5
Making Plans

Lunch was a cheerful affair. They all sat round the long, oval table in the sunny dining room, and feasted on cold chicken, ham salad, swiss cheese, and some of Mrs. Dunn's famous chocolate cake. When they had eaten all they could hold, and the grownups were sipping their coffee, Joe said, "That's one kind of ray I hope they never invent—an eating ray."

"Good heavens, Joe," said Mrs. Dunn. "What on earth made you think of that?"

"Oh, the Professor's new C-ray," Joe explained. "I just hope they never come up with anything to take the place of eating."

"I don't think you need worry," said the Professor, pulling out his old pipe. "Even if anyone succeeded in inventing such a device, I don't think most people would care for it. Food is too much fun."

"I agree," said Joe. "Boy! There are times when I get the feeling that science develops things that are supposed to be good for us, but that just make trouble."

Dr. Tresselt's blue eyes seemed to throw out sparks of amusement. "I know how you feel, Joe," he said. "But my stars, boy, nobody can be alive and never have any trouble! Being alive is just meeting troubles every day and overcoming them. Just to stand up straight against the pull of gravity is a fight, isn't it?"

"I think Joe would rather spend his days lying down," Irene giggled.

"Nothing wrong with that," Joe said. "You know, I can be as lively as anyone else, but there are times when I'd like to run away and live in a cave and be a hermit, and not have to—"

Danny's head snapped up. "Joe," he said, "you're brilliant."

"I am?" Joe raised his eyebrows.

"Yes, sir. I always knew it."

"You did?"

"That's a wonderful idea."

"It is, huh?" Joe blinked. "I am proud and

humble. Uh . . . which particular one of my many ideas are you talking about?''

"Why, mentioning the cave, of course. I'd forgotten all about it. How about going this afternoon?''

Dr. Tresselt had pricked up his ears. "Cave? What cave?''

"Oh, one Danny discovered,'' said Irene. "We were going to explore it this morning, when we found you. Danny made us leave it— he said it was more important to get you home.''

Professor Bullfinch opened his eyes wide at this, but before he could say anything, Dr. Tresselt said, crisply, "What's it like? Shallow? River running out of it? Carbonate of lime concretions?''

"Gee, Dr. Tresselt, I really don't know much about it,'' Danny answered. "You see, I found it last spring. I didn't have any light with me so I couldn't really explore it. But it didn't look shallow—it seemed to go 'way in. There's no river, and I don't know about carbonate of lime.''

Dr. Tresselt rose to his feet. "Let's go,'' he said.

"Hold on a minute, Alvin.'' Professor Bullfinch caught him by the wrist. "I absolutely forbid your dashing off into the hills this afternoon. I have arranged to introduce you to Herbert Jaffe, the chief of Midston's Geology Department—a great admirer of your work. He, in turn, is giving a faculty tea party for you, and he wants to take you around the school."

"Oh—heck!" said Dr. Tresselt, with a despairing look. "No way out of it?"

"Absolutely none. While you're here, you've got to meet some of these men. They are looking forward to it." The Professor tapped his chin with his pipestem, thoughtfully. "However, tomorrow—"

"Hooray!" Danny burst out. "An expedition!"

"Take it easy, Danny," cautioned the Professor. "I didn't say anything about an expedition. But we might just stroll up there in the morning, and—er—sort of glance inside. . . ."

"We can call it the Bullfinch-Tresselt Underground Expedition," said Irene. "We'd better make a list of all the things we'll need."

"Rope," Danny said, taking out his pencil. "And flashlights and spare batteries."

"A first-aid kit," Irene said.

"You'll need provisions, too," Joe put in.

"Aren't you coming?" Danny said.

"Oh, sure, you'll need somebody to help you eat them."

"Better put down warm clothing, too," said the Professor. "It'll be a lot chillier inside than out in the sun."

"I have another idea, Professor Bullfinch," said Danny. "You could bring along the C-ray. You said it ought to be tried out in the field. This would be a way of doing that, wouldn't it?"

"Fine," said the Professor. "A good thought. We ought to be able to check whether it picks up discontinuities in a homogenous mass."

"I'm almost certain it won't register fossil layers," Dr. Tresselt said, shaking his head. "I don't see how—"

"Tut, tut, my dear man," the Professor began.

Mrs. Dunn interrupted him. "Just a moment. Nobody's asked me what I think."

"Oh, Mom!" Danny cried. "Please say we can go. *Please*."

"Hmmm. I don't know."

"I really don't think there will be any danger," said the Professor. "In the first place, both Alvin and I have had considerable experience in speleology."

"It's not your spelling I'm worried about," Mrs. Dunn said.

"Speleology is the scientific study of caves,"

Professor Bullfinch smiled. "Both of us have done a good deal of caving, and we'll take all the necessary precautions. In the second place, I feel that Danny deserves this trip. You may not realize it, but this morning he did something that showed great strength of character. You heard what Irene said: he was about to explore the cave, but then he saw to it that Tresselt got here, instead. I don't think Dr. Tresselt would have given up an interesting project like that. I'm not even sure I'd have done so myself."

"It's a good thing he didn't mention it this morning," Dr. Tresselt said, with a chuckle. "I probably would have camped on the spot."

"That's what I mean," Mrs. Dunn said, drily. "I'm not too worried about Danny. He knows how to take care of himself, and I'm sure I can trust him to be cautious. It's you two grownups I'm worried about."

"Us?" The Professor looked blank.

"Just so. You're liable to get these youngsters into that cave and then start one of your investigations and forget all about them. They might manage to get home—but will you?"

The Professor and Dr. Tresselt looked at each other and then at Mrs. Dunn. They both had rather foolish expressions, like overgrown schoolboys being scolded by the teacher.

Irene put in, "Oh, Mrs. Dunn, we'll promise to take care of them and see to it that they don't get into trouble."

Mrs. Dunn's eyes twinkled, and she got up and began to clear the table. "Well," she said, "I'll give my permission for Danny to go, in that case."

"I'm going home right now," said Irene, jumping up, "and ask my mother, but if you say it's all right, she will too."

"Okay," Danny said, picking up a pile of dishes to take to the kitchen. "Then come back. You too, Joe. We've got lots of plans to make and things to get ready for tomorrow. The Bullfinch-Tresselt Underground Expedition is on its way!"

6
Slide into Darkness

Although the night was damp and cloudy, the morning dawned bright and clear and the expedition hiked up through the woods under a brilliant sky. As Danny remarked, it wouldn't make much difference to them what kind of day it was once they got underground, but it raised their spirits immensely before they started.

They found the way without difficulty, following Irene's blazed trail. As they approached the big oak tree, Dr. Tresselt stopped and pointed to a deep gully cut in the earth like a wagon road.

"Many of these caves in limestone hills were carved out by flowing streams," he said. "That gully shows where the stream may once have come out.''

"And there's the cave itself," Danny cried, in excitement.

They could see that the oak tree stood on a rocky point formed by two great slabs leaning against each other. Below was a black opening, like the entrance to a teepee. They climbed up to it, and then paused to pull on sweaters or heavy jackets.

They were all variously loaded down. Dr. Tresselt carried a powerful battery lamp belonging to the Professor; Professor Bullfinch had another such lamp and his C-ray; the three young people each wore a knapsack and carried a good flashlight. Irene had a first-aid kit in her pack, and spare batteries for all the different lamps. Joe's knapsack was stuffed with sandwiches, chocolate bars, and cookies. Danny opened his pack and took out a square metal box with a handle at the top, a pair of earphones, and what looked like a microphone on a cable attached to it.

"Well, well," said Dr. Tresselt. "A Geiger-Müller counter, eh? Planning to do a little prospecting for uranium?''

"I doubt there's any around here, Danny," said the Professor, gravely.

"It's not for that at all," Danny replied,

42

"This is for finding our way back."

checking over the instrument and replacing it in his pack. "But since this is a scientific expedition, we ought to do the whole thing scientifically. So this is for finding our way back."

"I don't think I quite understand," the Professor said. "How is a Geiger counter going to help?"

"Well, I borrowed this from Professor Blum, in the Physics Department, yesterday," Danny said. "And I also got from him some thorium nitrate crystals. They're mildly radioactive, you know, and they'll register on the counter and make it click rapidly. I've got 'em in this little box. Every time we come to a place where there's more than one way to go, I'll drop a few of them. Then, when we come back, we can pick up our trail with the counter. See?"

The Professor rubbed his bald head. "I see. But wouldn't it have been easier if you had just brought along a small can of white paint and a brush?"

"Easier?" Danny shook his head, scornfully. "Gosh, no! Opening and closing a can of sloppy paint? And messing around with a brush?"

"As it happens, I brought along a piece of chalk," Dr. Tresselt observed, mildly.

"Chalk? But gosh, Dr. Tresselt," Danny wailed, "that isn't scientific at all!"

"All right," said Professor Bullfinch. "We'll let you do it your way, Dan, since you've made such careful preparations. Now, are we all set?"

"Right!" said Dr. Tresselt.

"I'm ready," said Joe. He took a notebook and a pencil out of his pocket. "Ten A.M. The expedition arrived at the cave entrance and prepared to make its way to the very center of the earth."

"Sounds exciting," said the Professor. "Only I don't think we'll be going that far down."

"It's what they call 'artistic license,'" Joe explained. "I've decided to write a report about the trip for the school magazine, and I have to make it seem dangerous even if it isn't." He gulped nervously. "Anyway, I sure hope it isn't."

"I'm ready," said Irene. She jingled the charm bracelet, which this morning she was wearing on her wrist. "I'm going to see if I can find something interesting to represent geology on my bracelet."

"Let's go, then," said the Professor.

He stepped forward, snapping on his lamp.

Danny was right at his heels, and the others pressed close behind.

They stood in a rock chamber with high, arching walls. Under the beams of their lights the wall shone like glass, and here and there clusters of white crystals flashed out. The floor was covered with loose stone and gravel. The ceiling, arched and craggy, sloped down toward the back of the cave where it was lost in darkness.

Dr. Tresselt bent and picked up what looked like a round, white pebble. "Carbonate of lime," he said. "The result of the passage of water through the limestone."

Irene and Joe drew close to look. Danny, after a glance, went to the back of the cave. "Professor Bullfinch," he called, his voice echoing in the chamber. "There's an opening here. Plenty big enough for you to stand up in."

The Professor hastened to join him, and together they shone their lights into the space. "It's a real tunnel, all right," he said.

Its floor slanted steeply downward, and was covered with loose gravel. The Professor took a cautious step or two, and then said, "I can hear something trickling. There may be a stream down there."

"Oh, boy!" Danny said. "A secret underground river!"

He darted forward. His foot slipped in the gravel, and he lost his balance. He grabbed for the nearest support, which happened to be the front of the Professor's jacket.

The Professor went plunging down the slope, with Danny clinging to him. Somehow they managed to keep from falling. Sliding and swaying, they raced downward, their lights darting crazily as they waved their arms to keep their balance. Then, all at once, they hit a patch of wet clay.

The Professor's heels went out from under him.

"I can't—" he yelled.

Thump! Down he went, with Dan on top of him.

There was a long pause. At last, in a muffled voice, he finished: "—keep my balance. Would you mind taking your elbow out of my ear, Dan?"

7
The Underground Waterfall

They disentangled themselves and got to their feet. The back of the Professor's coat was covered with blue clay, which Danny tried vainly to wipe off.

"I'm awfully sorry," the boy said. "It was all my fault. I shouldn't have rushed out ahead of you like that."

The Professor shook his head. "There are times when you are rather—uh—sudden, Dan," he said, mildly. "However, this gravel is tricky stuff. And in cave exploring, I suppose we must expect a few spills."

Fortunately, their lights weren't damaged. The Professor looked about for his C-ray. It lay close at hand, one corner buried in soft clay.

"It seems to be all right," said the Professor, examining it. "I hope none of the tubes have been broken."

He was about to snap it on and try it, when from the cave above them came a hail from Dr. Tresselt.

"Ahoy, Bullfinch! Are you down there?"

The Professor turned back and shouted, "Yes! Come on down."

Gravel began rattling along the slope and within a few moments their friends had joined them.

Dr. Tresselt said, "Do you really think it was wise, Euclid, to go on ahead without telling the rest of us where you were going?"

"Don't be annoyed, my dear chap," the Professor replied. "In theory you are absolutely correct, but this was a case where theory and practice didn't go together. I didn't even have time to yell 'Help!' "

Danny had been examining their surroundings, and he now broke in, "You were right, Professor. There is a stream."

They crowded round him. The clay bank ended in a flat strand of stone, below which flowed a shallow river some nine or ten feet wide. Smooth boulders stuck up out of it, and on its other shore rose a wall of glistening rock.

The water was black in the lamplight, but when Joe shone the beam of his flashlight directly into it they could see that it was as clear as glass.

"Hey, there are fish in this stream," Joe said. "But golly, they look awfully pale. Aren't they well?"

"They're just bleached out from living in the dark," Irene said, leaning over to watch the slender white forms that darted in and out of the circle of light. "Do you think they're blind, too, Dr. Tresselt?"

The geologist nodded. "Possibly," he said. He wasn't looking into the water, however, but at the walls of the cavern. "You know," he went on, "I think we are looking at the thing which dug out these caves in the first place."

"We are?" Danny cried. "Where is it?"

"A machine?" said Joe. "Or a prehistoric monster?"

"A kind of prehistoric monster," Dr. Tresselt chuckled. "There it is—right at your feet."

Joe jumped back.

"I know what you mean," said Danny, grinning. "The river!"

"Just so. The river cut its way through the soft limestone—of course, when I say 'soft' I mean that only in terms of other rocks—during millions of years, eating it away and making a bigger and bigger passage for itself.''

"Then why doesn't it still come out at the upper cave, where we entered?" Danny asked. "We saw the dry bed where it used to be, remember. What made it stop running up there?"

"I think there must have been other streams tunneling below it," Dr. Tresselt replied. "Or possibly an earthquake shifted the rock. Hard to say. Whatever the reason was, the bed of the river collapsed and the stream level dropped."

"Where do you think it comes out now?" Irene said. "Somewhere in the valley?"

"Maybe at the reservoir," Danny suggested.

Dr. Tresselt flashed his light, first down the stream, then up. "It's difficult to say. It could come out a long way below Midston." He walked a little way upstream and paused. "Shh! Don't I hear something?"

They cocked their heads. At last, Irene said, "I can hear a kind of hollow, roaring sound."

"Yes, so can I," said Danny.

"A waterfall?" asked Professor Bullfinch.

"I wouldn't be surprised," Dr. Tresselt answered.

"Let's go see," Danny said. And before the

others could answer, he was already trotting along the flat stone shore toward the distant sound.

"Hey, wait!" called Joe. "Maybe it's too risky. Maybe we'll be washed away. Maybe it's—oh, what's the use?" he finished, shrugging. "Let's go."

"Yes, since we've come this far," the Professor said, smiling, "I must say, I wouldn't mind seeing an underground waterfall myself. If that's what it really is."

Irene and Joe soon caught up with Danny and the three made their way along the bank of the river, side by side. The water clucked and gurgled softly. Joe kept shining his light into it, and reflections shot up and sparkled from the walls and roof.

"What I'd like to do," Danny said, "is bring a boat here and travel right down the river. Wouldn't that be fun?"

"Fun?" Joe snorted. "We'd probably end up coming out of somebody's water faucet."

"Oh, Joe. You're always looking on the dark side of things," Irene protested.

"Well, what of it?" Joe gestured with his light at the gloomy cavern around them. "Where else *would* you look, down here?"

"I suppose the chances are that it might be impossible to get all the way downstream,"

Irene said. "The tunnel might get too low for a boat to get through. Or the water might drop down deeper and deeper."

"To the center of the earth," Joe muttered. "And then we'd be boiled to death. Boiled Joe with cave sauce. What a way to end!"

Danny laughed. "Well, don't start planning your own menu, Joe. We haven't even got a boat."

Joe shook his head. "If I know you, you'll probably invent one before we get out of here," he said. "Nothing but trouble."

The passage grew smaller so that they now had to go in single file. Columns of stone, some of them polished and smooth, rose before them and they had to pick their way slowly. The air grew damp and a cool, faint breeze touched their faces. The roaring, rushing noise was so loud it seemed to shake the very rocks.

All at once Danny stopped, so abruptly that Irene bumped into him. She looked over his shoulder. Then she turned to Joe. "Look at this!" She had to yell to make herself heard, even though he was right behind her.

In the light of their combined torches, a magical sight appeared. A curtain of diamonds was strung before them. Its foot was white foam in which floated rainbow-colored bubbles the size of soup bowls. It was not very high, but it had a majestic look, pouring from the roof of the cave and winding away between the ledges of shining stone.

"It's like fairyland," Irene said. The boys nodded soberly.

As they stood gazing in wonder, the two men caught up with them. They, too, stared at the lovely waterfall in silence for a long time.

The Professor gave a long sigh. He shone his flashlight along the top of the falls, and they could see that the rocky roof came down almost to the water. The walls closed in, too, on either side.

"It looks as though this is the end of the trip," he said. "This is as far as we can go."

8
The Bridge
of Stone

They all moved back a little way to avoid the spray which was beginning to soak them, and sat down on a ledge from which they could look about in comfort. Professor Bullfinch pointed to the roof.

"Icicles!" Joe exclaimed.

The roof here was composed of flat slabs of stone, veined with darker green and pale blue. From it hung hundreds of what appeared to be pointing fingers, some of them a few inches long, some nearly a foot.

"Stalactites," Danny said. "I've read about them. They're formed by water dripping from above, aren't they, Professor?"

"Yes. The water seeps through minerals and leaves deposits of them as it evaporates. It may take about ten years for an inch-long stalactite of the thickness of those on the roof to form. Thicker ones may take longer. Those, for instance—''

He pointed with his lamp at the wall, some distance away and to one side of the waterfall. They saw several immense stalactites hanging down, perhaps two feet thick and as tall as a man.

''Those may have taken a hundred thousand years to form,'' said the Professor.

''Whew! The ones up on the ceiling are babies, then,'' Joe said. ''Thirty- or forty-year-old babies.''

''Yes. Probably they haven't grown longer because there is a slight air current here caused by the rush of the falls. That would make the dripping water evaporate too quickly.''

Danny got up. ''I'd like to look at those big stalactites,'' he said. He wandered off, his light throwing strange shadows from the stone and water.

Joe pointed his own flashlight in Danny's direction. ''Look, Professor,'' he said. ''There's an upside-down stalactite. One that got mixed up and grew the wrong way.''

A pointed column grew out of the floor not far from where Danny was at that moment walking. It was almost as high as the boy himself, with a dazzling white streak down the side of it, like snow on a thin, steep mountain.

"Ah, that kind we call stalagmites," said Dr. Tresselt. "They are caused by water dropping on the floor and building secretions of minerals from the ground up."

As he spoke, Danny let out a yell. His voice echoed in the chamber above the noise of the water.

Joe sprang to his feet. "A stalactite's got him!" he said.

The others stood up, too. They could see Danny waving his light back and forth, as if to signal them.

"I believe he's found something," said the Professor.

He had, indeed, found something. When the others joined him, he pointed triumphantly. Behind the stalactites, which hung almost to the floor, was an opening. It was very small, but one person at a time could enter it on hands and knees.

"It gets bigger after a little way," he said. "If you shine your light in, you can see that it's a kind of split in the rock, and there's a ledge that goes up, almost like a stairway."

Dr. Tresselt immediately bent over to peer into the opening. "Ah, yes, I see," he said. "Well, well. A most interesting formation. . . ."

He crawled through. At once, Danny followed.

The Professor said, doubtfully, "I wonder if we ought to wait—"

Dan's face reappeared in the entrance. "Gosh, come on," he cried. "It's terrific! All sparkling—!"

Professor Bullfinch nodded. "Very well," he said. "I suppose we can push on for a while longer. Go on, Irene, and you, Joe. I'll bring up the rear."

The ledge mounted steeply through a high, narrow crack in the stone. It was jagged and slippery, but they could find foothold enough to keep going up. The sides were streaked with white crystals that twinkled and flashed like snow under their lamps. They climbed for about five minutes, and then Dr. Tresselt, still in the lead, called back, "Be careful when you get up here."

"What have you found, Alvin?" shouted the Professor.

"The ledge widens up here," replied the geologist, "but one wall opens out. You'll see when you get here. Just keep to the left and watch your step."

Danny clambered up the last few yards that separated him from where the geologist was standing. The rock face on his right ended in empty space. The ledge broadened out and sloped slightly inward, and there was enough room for him to stand safely beside Dr. Tresselt. As the others came up, Dr. Tresselt flashed his light out into the dark void on their right.

"There's our river again," he remarked.

Some twenty feet below where they stood was the water, a black mirror vanishing into a cleft in the stone.

"You see, Dan?" said Irene. "That's one reason it might be hard to get downstream in a boat. The river keeps going into tunnels like that one, where there wouldn't be room for a boat to stay on the surface."

"You could use a submarine," Danny said. "Or a skin-diver's outfit. Don't they sometimes do that, Dr. Tresselt?"

"Yes," said the geologist. "In a place in England which has the rather odd name of Wooky Hole, skin-divers have managed to get to almost a dozen caves which are strung out along an underground river, something like this one."

Danny said, "The ledge is still here, and it's almost as wide as a sidewalk. Let's keep going."

The Professor pulled out his watch and glanced at it. "We've been underground for almost an hour,'' he said. ''I know we ought to turn back but I must confess I find this absolutely fascinating. What do you say, Alvin?''

''Oh, let's go on for a bit,'' said the geologist, turning to examine the wall behind them. ''I'd like to see some more of these caves. You know, I suspect that a certain amount of mud was carried through here at one time. Look, there are some darker deposits in the limestone.''

He chipped a few bits out with the sharp pickend of his hammer, and then moved on after the young people.

Danny had taken the lead, and he went along boldly, looking about with great interest. The ledge began to grow narrower. The walls fell away on either side and he found himself in a larger cavern, the roof of which vanished into darkness. The ledge ended at a gap, some nine feet wide and tapering toward the bottom, far below, where the river still trickled. The gap looked as though a giant had split the rock with his ax. On its other side was a fairly wide shelf, and then the mouth of another tunnel. The gap was spanned by a mass of rubble which had fallen from the roof and was jammed into the triangular space, and across the top of it, like a rude bridge, lay a slab of solid stone about two feet wide and several inches thick.

Irene looked doubtfully at the block of stone. "What do you think, Dan?" she asked. "Will it hold us? Can we get across?"

Danny scratched his freckled nose. "It's got to," he said. "I don't want to go back until we've seen as much as we can."

He took off his knapsack, swung it by the straps and threw it across to the shelf on the other side. "There," he said. "Now I've *got* to get across."

He stepped cautiously out on the slab.

"Oooh, I can't look," said Joe.

Dan held his breath, but nothing happened. Then he walked lightly and swiftly the rest of the way until he was standing beside his pack.

"It's easy," he called. "Come ahead."

Irene tossed her own pack over to him, and walked across, trying not to look down.

Joe said, "You know, I don't really want to do this. Couldn't I just wait here and sort of think about things while you're exploring?"

"What about those notes you're taking for the story you're going to write?" said Danny. "Are you going to say, 'The expedition descended into the depths and left me behind because I was scared'?"

"Not a bad idea," groaned Joe. "Oh, all right. Catch the pack."

He threw it over and Danny put it beside the

others. Then Joe, gritting his teeth, made the crossing.

As soon as he had done so, he pulled out his notebook. Holding it on his knee, with his flashlight tucked under his chin, he began to write.

Danny looked over his shoulder.

"What is he saying?" Irene asked.

Joe read aloud: "At eleven-fifteen A.M. I heroically led the expedition across an impassable bridge."

"I have a feeling there's something wrong with that sentence," Irene giggled.

Just then, the two scientists emerged on the ledge on the other side of the gap.

They were deep in talk. Danny was about to call out to them. Before he could do so, however, and without for a moment hesitating or stopping their conversation, Dr. Tresselt marched right out on the bridge, and the Professor followed at his heels. Neither of the men seemed to notice anything out of the ordinary, so absorbed were they in their discussion.

"—the lime carbonate concretions would seem to indicate a steady flow of water down that fissure," Dr. Tresselt was saying.

"Perhaps," replied the Professor. "On the other hand, isn't it possible that it represents

With a crash the whole mass collapsed.

a fracture, possibly of seismologic origin, and that the concretions—"

At this instant, there was a faint rumbling sound.

"Hmm," said Dr. Tresselt. "Did you hear that? Sounded like rock falling."

The slab on which they stood settled visibly.

"An earthquake, perhaps?" said the Professor. "It appeared to me that the stone moved beneath my feet."

They both looked down.

"This is most interesting," Dr. Tresselt said, thoughtfully. "We appear to be standing on a mass of loose rubble. I have a feeling that our combined weights are unsettling it."

"I think, my dear Alvin," said the Professor, "that we had better get off as quickly as—"

And suddenly, everything happened at once. Irene uttered a scream. The two men were only a short distance from the shelf on which the young people were standing, and they both gave tremendous leaps. Joe grabbed Dr. Tresselt's arm, and Danny caught the Professor. They were safe. But those jumps had given the slab a jolt which was too much for the loose rocks beneath. With a slow, ponderous crash, the whole mass collapsed.

9
A Loss and
a Decision

The five stood huddled together, gazing at each other in dismay. Then they turned their lamps into the gap at their feet. Dust rose like smoke through the beams of light, but they could see clearly enough what had happened. The stones had sunk carrying the slab of rock with them, and it now lay wedged across the sloping walls of the chasm a good ten feet below.

"I think," said the Professor, "that that's as far as it will fall. If we have some rope with us we can get down to it."

"We've got lots of rope," Danny said. "But I wonder if it's really firm. It would be awful to get down on it and have it slide another fifty feet, or break in half."

"There's also the problem of getting up the other side," said Dr. Tresselt, solemnly.

Professor Bullfinch took out his pipe and lit it with a preoccupied air. "It looks as though we have a serious problem on our hands. In the first place, how much rope have we actually got?"

"I have fifty feet of clothesline in my pack," Danny answered. "Irene has some, too."

"Only about ten feet," she said. "It's all my mother could spare."

"Hmm. That should be enough." The Professor blew out a plume of smoke. "I think the four of you could hold me on that line and lower me to the slab. If it seemed secure, one of the boys could come down and stand on my shoulders—Joe, I imagine, would be a bit lighter than Danny. He could get up to the top of the other side. There are several stalagmites over there to which a piece of line could be fastened, and we could all climb up."

"There's one thing against that, Euclid," said Dr. Tresselt. "It's a dangerous stunt, balancing a boy on your shoulders, on a narrow slab of rock like that."

"There's another thing against it," Joe put in. "Me. I'm against it."

"I'll do it, Professor," Danny said. "And

I'll bet I don't weigh much more than Joe does. He's just stretched out more than I am.''

"We may have to do that as a last resort,'' said the Professor. ''However, there is another alternative. We can go on through this tunnel in the hope of finding another way out. I can think of several caves—Howe Caverns, in New York State, for example—which have two or more entrances. It is just possible that there's a way out on the other side of Sugarloaf.''

"It's a slim chance,'' said Dr. Tresselt. ''However, I think we ought to take it. If we can't find another way, we can always return here and try your acrobatic method.''

"Very well. Then let's get started,'' the Professor said. ''How are the lights? Still holding up?''

"Still bright enough,'' said Dr. Tresselt. ''A good thing we didn't drop ours when we had to jump.''

They bent to pick up their things. Suddenly, Joe let out a howl.

"Great heavens!'' exclaimed the Professor. ''What's the matter?''

"Are you hurt?'' said Irene.

Joe was flashing his light here and there, and making so much noise that he didn't hear them. Dr. Tresselt seized his arm.

"Stop!" shouted the geologist. "Be quiet! Now, for goodness' sake, tell us what's wrong so that we can help you."

"You can't help me," groaned Joe. "Nobody can help me."

Danny patted his friend on the back. "Tell us, Joe," he begged. "I'm sure the Professor and Dr. Tresselt between them can do something."

"They've already done it," Joe said, growing somewhat quieter.

"What?"

"When they jumped, I caught Dr. Tresselt's arms and we staggered backward. You and the Professor fell against us. Somebody's foot must have hit my knapsack and knocked it off the ledge. It's gone!"

There was silence for a moment. Then Irene said, "Oh, Joe! All that yelling—? You can always get another knapsack. You can have mine if it will make you feel better."

"What good is yours?" said Joe. "All the food was in mine—all except a couple of chocolate bars I've got in my pocket. We'll starve!"

The Professor burst into laughter. Dr. Tresselt said, "I don't really think we'll be here long enough to starve, Joe. I'm sure we can either find another way out, or get back somehow across this gap."

"You don't know me," Joe said, tragically. "I can starve in a minute."

"Buck up, my lad," said Professor Bullfinch, cheerfully. "Your hunger will give us a further reason for escaping. Meanwhile, put up with it as best you can."

Joe nodded. After a moment's thought, he took out his notebook and wrote, " 'Weak, tottering, and famished though I was, I divided the last of my food with my friends, and we pressed on.' There. A noble act like that makes me feel much better." He pulled two candy bars from his pocket and offered them around.

They broke off bits of the chocolate and munched them. Feeling much refreshed, Danny and Irene slung their knapsacks on their backs, and Joe offered to carry the C-ray for a while. Then Dr. Tresselt, holding his lantern high, stepped forward.

10
Danny in the Dark

The shelf ended in a wall of stone, covered with folds and ripples made by the minerals washing down from the earth above. It looked like a curtain, but shone glassily where their lights struck it. A wide opening led them into another tunnel, and they began to descend again. Spikes and spires rose about them, and stalactites of all sizes hung from above.

Danny said, "We ought to name these places as we go through them. Look there—those stalactites are like a row of teeth. We could call this the Dragon's Mouth."

"Yes, what we really need is to make a map," Irene suggested.

"What for?" said Joe. "If we ever get out

of here, I won't need a map because I won't come back."

"Why, Joe, this is a marvelous discovery," Irene said. "These caves might become famous, like Luray Caverns or Mammoth Cave. People would come from all over America to see them."

"Gee, I never thought of that," said Joe, enthusiastically. "Why, we could make a fortune. I can see it now: *Pearson, Dunn, Miller, Bullfinch & Tresselt Caverns*. ADMISSION ONE DOLLAR. Maybe we could just call them the Pearson Caverns, for short. Oh, boy! First, I'll buy a gold-plated bicycle—"

"Hold on a minute, Joe," chuckled the Professor. "Don't get too excited. In the first place, we don't own this land. It belongs to the town. However, I should think Irene is right in one way. These caves are a real discovery. Midston should be grateful to you three. You might even get jobs as guides, if the caves should ever be opened to the public. However, before that happens, we have to find our way out of here."

"Yes, I almost forgot about that," sighed Joe. "Why did you have to remind me?"

"Have you been dropping the radioactive material as we go, Danny?" Irene asked.

"No, not yet," said Dan, climbing around

a stalagmite that rose like a tree in the center of the tunnel. "So far, there's been no chance of missing the way back. But it looks as though I'll be using it soon."

"Why?"

"The way divides up ahead. I can see another tunnel leading off to the left."

"Quite right," said Dr. Tresselt. "Now, the question is, which one do we take?"

They drew together, staring at the fork. The Professor said, "Perhaps we ought to send a scout a little way down to see what it's like."

"I'll go," Danny cried eagerly, and without waiting for permission he darted ahead into the branching tunnel.

"Just a minute—" the Professor began, but the boy was already out of sight around an angle of rock.

This tunnel twisted back and forth, and it was very narrow, so narrow that Dan could reach out and touch the walls on either hand. They were different, too, from those in the passage he had just left: they were streaked here and there with dark red, as ominous as blood. There were no stone icicles or pillars, only the flat floor underfoot, and the cramped, winding walls that came together high above.

Danny began to feel a trifle uneasy. He had started off full of excitement, but now that he was alone he was very conscious of the silence. It was absolute silence, in which there was only the soft padding of his footsteps. When he stopped for a moment, he was surprised to hear a dull pounding. It took him a few seconds to realize that it was the beating of his own pulses. He whistled a few notes, but they died away amongst the solid stone, and he soon gave it up; it made him feel even lonelier. He went on and the walls began to close together. The passageway grew narrower still and at last there was only a small crack, just barely wide enough for him to squeeze through.

He stood still. The thumping of his heart shook his whole body, and his flashlight trembled in his hand. Maybe I'd better turn back right now, he thought.

Then he pulled himself together. No! he said to himself. I volunteered for this, and shoved on in here even though the Professor tried to stop me. I'll go on until I *have* to stop.

He took a long breath and went on. Soon, he had to turn sideways, and the rough stone scraped his back and chest, bunching up the leather jacket he was wearing. He could feel it pull and scrape on projections of stone.

All at once, there was nothing under his right foot.

Nothing! Even as the thought flashed through

his mind, his foot went down into empty air and he threw out his right hand to try to find some support. His flashlight went whirling away, and vanished into a huge black space, and in the same instant he realized that he was not going to fall. He was wedged tightly between the rocks by the folds of his jacket, and this held him securely in place.

He was too frightened even to yell. He just stood still, clinging to a point of stone with his left hand, his breath caught in his throat. At the same time, his mind was busy counting: *one, two, three, four, five* . . . and then he heard the faint clatter as his flashlight hit bottom somewhere far below.

He gulped. Then he calmed himself a little and got his right foot back on the firm rock. He inched himself away from that dreadful edge which he could no longer see. He was in absolute pitch darkness, a kind of darkness he had never experienced before, not even when he had once been shut in a closet by accident. This was a blackness which had never known any light, and he felt as if he were being crushed by it. Now, he was thankful that the walls were so close together. He put a hand on either wall and walked back the way he had come, trying not to give way to panic and break into a run. He kept telling himself that he would see his friends any minute. In spite of the coolness of the air he was drenched with sweat and had to keep wiping his eyes on his sleeve.

The passage seemed to go on forever. But just as he was beginning to feel that he really couldn't bear it any longer and would have to start yelling for help, he saw a pale glow ahead. It grew brighter, and then he could hear the happy sound of voices.

He came out into the light of his friends' lanterns and stood there blinking.

"Well, it's about time," said the Professor, speaking in what was, for him, a rather severe tone. "Please, Danny, don't ever rush off like that again. You must learn to control your impulses, at least while we're still in these caves."

Danny tried to get his breathing back to normal again. At length he said, "I'm—I'm sorry. I know it was dopy. I won't do it again."

"What about the tunnel?" asked Dr. Tresselt. "Any good?"

Danny mopped his face. "No good to anybody," he said, with a shudder. "Just no good at all."

"We were about to follow you," said the Professor. "Good heavens! Did you know that the back of your jacket is torn?" He looked more closely at the boy. "And you're as white as a sheet. Danny! What happened? What did you find?"

"Nothing."

"Nothing?"

"That's right. The passage goes on until it turns into a lemon squeezer, and then it becomes—nothing. Just air. Listen, Professor Bullfinch, what's the formula for a free-falling body?"

The Professor, with a slightly puzzled air, replied, "$s = \frac{1}{2}gt^2$."

Danny did a quick calculation in his head. "It took my flashlight five seconds to fall," he said. "So that pit is about four hundred feet deep. All I have to say," he finished, with a shudder, "is that it's a good thing I was wearing this heavy leather jacket and not a light, thin sweater."

He told them the whole story, and when he was done Professor Bullfinch said, gravely, "A very lucky escape, my boy. That settles it; from now on we must all keep together. There must be no dashing off alone. Danny, I've told you several times that you must learn not to be so headstrong. A scientist must consider every step carefully before he moves, and if you expect to live to become a scientist—"

"Don't worry, Professor," Danny said.

"I'm not going to forget that moment in a hurry. When my foot just went into empty air—ugh!"

"Good." Professor Bullfinch smiled affectionately at the boy. "Now, let's go on. I'll walk in front, this time."

11
The Glittering Cave

Danny carefully laid a trail of thorium nitrate crystals so that he would be able to find the right path with his Geiger counter on the way back. As they were waiting, Dr. Tresselt tapped Professor Bullfinch on the arm.

"Euclid," he said, "before we go on, I'd like to take a look at those reddish streaks Danny described, on the walls of this branch tunnel."

The Professor looked doubtful. "Do you think it's wise?"

"I'll only go a little way in. As a matter of fact," said Dr. Tresselt, "why don't you come with me, and bring that C-ray? This might be a good time to try it. I have an idea about those streaks, and your device, if it works, might be helpful.''

They entered the branch tunnel, and when they had gone round the first sharp angle of the rock, Dr. Tresselt pulled out his hammer and a small chisel. Professor Bullfinch held the light up for him, and the geologist examined the wall carefully. Then he chipped out a few pieces of the red material.

''I think this may be clay,'' he said. ''Or perhaps mud, with a high percentage of iron oxides. It's embedded in the limestone. What does that suggest to you?''

Joe, who was peering over the Professor's shoulder, said, "Mud pies."

The Professor snorted. "Not exactly. The river?"

"Just so," Dr. Tresselt agreed. "It looks very much as though there had once been another stream running through here, carrying mud in with it. Or. . . ." He paused, tapping his hammer pensively against the wall.

"Or?"

"I wonder if mud could have been washed in by the flooding of a river outside? Then, when the water subsided, the mud would remain and petrify. Much later, another stream might have risen in the mountain and begun to make its way through here, cutting away the solid mud and leaving these traces. Then that stream, too, vanished in its turn."

The Professor nodded. "I see. Let's try the C-ray. It may show us some fossils in the mud."

It was difficult to work in that narrow space, but they got the machine braced on top of one of the knapsacks and the Professor turned it on. It hummed faintly, and the screen lit up. They saw a blurred tangle of vague shadows against the glow.

"Not very clear, is it?" said Dr. Tresselt.

The Professor turned a knob. Nothing happened. He began fussing with dials and snapping switches on and off, muttering to himself as he did so. Still, they could see nothing but those shadowy shapes, like the trailing edges of clouds.

"Too bad," said Dr. Tresselt. "But I was afraid it wouldn't operate properly on stone."

Professor Bullfinch sighed, and snapped off the C-ray.

"Well," said Irene, as she picked up her pack again, "it's a good thing there isn't any fossil Joe inside that wall, stealing a stone chicken leg."

"Even a stone chicken leg wouldn't be so bad," Joe grumbled.

Dr. Tresselt flashed his light down the tunnel. "I'd like to follow this to the end," he said, wistfully.

"Not today, Alvin," said the Professor. "In the first place, if Dan was right you couldn't squeeze through the last part of it."

"And a good thing, too," said Danny, with a shiver.

"But it's important," said the geologist.

"It's more important for us to find a way out," the Professor said.

"Mm. Yes. Well, I'm pretty sure that water came in here from another source," said Dr.

Tresselt. "Not from the river we followed. So if we keep going, we have a good chance of finding another way out—the place where that water entered."

They returned to the main tunnel. Joe took the C-ray and let Danny carry his flashlight. Off they went again, with the Professor in the lead.

The tunnel began to grow smaller. The roof lowered, the walls drew in, and they had to go single-file once more. The Professor picked his way carefully, climbing over rough places and worming his way around and over bulges in the rocky walls. Suddenly, he stopped short.

Danny, who was behind him, said, "What's the matter, Professor?"

"Nothing's the matter," he answered. "But this is well worth seeing."

"What is?"

"Spectacular," the Professor went on, without budging. "Truly beautiful."

"Professor Bullfinch!" Danny yelled.

"Eh? What's the matter?"

"You keep talking about how beautiful something is, but we can't see a thing unless you move out of the way."

"Oh, sorry," laughed the Professor, and stepped forward. The others followed him at once. They found themselves standing in an immense cavern, far larger than anything they had yet seen.

They saw at once why the Professor had exclaimed as he did. Their lamps seemed to flash from countless jewels, as they played them about the walls. From the high arched ceiling hung thick stalactites with rippled surfaces, some of them dark red, or brown, or jade green. Weird shapes rose all about them: rocks banded with many colors, worn and cut by water that had flowed through this chamber and carved it out countless millions of years before. Everywhere were crystals which sparkled like snow in the beams of the lights, or polished surfaces beaded with moisture, and as they stood silently gazing about them they heard the steady dripping of water from a dozen places, water that would slowly form more stalactites and stalagmites.

"Jumping catfish!" breathed Joe at last.

"I agree with you," said the Professor. "There doesn't seem to be much else to say."

12

"The Whole Cave Is Radioactive!"

The five explorers advanced into the center of the cave. Here, the floor rose in a series of flat shelves, or rather, steps, to a kind of platform some six or seven feet high. Above this hung three huge stalactites, almost touching the top of it. Dr. Tresselt climbed up on the platform and placed his light behind one of the stalactites. They could see the light shining right through the translucent stone as if it were some kind of thick glass, now yellow, then as he moved the lamp, a faint rose color.

"Listen," he said, and tapped the stalactite with his hammer, gently. A deep-toned note boomed through the cavern, like a great bell.

"Gee, what a church this would make," Joe

said, admiringly. "It's got everything—even an altar and a bell."

They began wandering about the cavern, feasting their eyes on its wonders. They found a rock that looked like the face of an old witch, and another that had been worn into the shape of a roaring lion. They found, too, that there were a number of other tunnels leading out of this cave as if it were some central hall in an ancient castle, with all its passageways running off in every direction. They were of all sizes, some barely large enough for a man to creep into, some larger than the front door of a house.

"Let's sit down and rest for a bit," the Professor said, after some moments.

They made themselves as comfortable as they could on the steps of what they called the "Altar," and Joe pulled out a bag of peanuts.

"I found these when we were looking through our pockets a while ago," he said, proudly. "Just let me count them. . . ."

"A peanut counter!" giggled Irene. "Almost as good as a Geiger counter."

"Better," said Joe. "We've got to ration ourselves, though. Let's see, five apiece and two left over. Hmm. Professor Bullfinch, what's the formula for dividing two peanuts among five people?"

"Much too complicated, Joe," said the Professor soberly. "Why don't you simply split them in half. Each of you young people take one half, and Dr. Tresselt and I will divide the remaining half between us."

Dr. Tresselt nodded. "We aren't quite as hungry as you are, I'm sure."

They ate their peanuts, with solemn and quiet pleasure.

"How quiet it is," Danny said, digging in his knapsack for the canteen full of water he had brought. "You don't realize how scary it is, having a whole mountain on top of you, until you're in the dark as I was in that tunnel, or when you begin hearing the silence."

"I didn't know you could hear silence," said Irene.

"Then just listen."

They sat still, and Danny added, "Put out the flashlights for a minute."

In the dark, they understood what he meant. All the familiar noises of the upper world were gone: the wind, the rustle of branches or leaves, the chirping of birds, the sounds of automobiles and doors slamming, and people laughing. There was nothing but the faint tinkle of droplets of water, each drop like a distant musical chime, and each one pursued by tiny echoes. Then, after such a note had sounded there would be a long and empty quiet in which

The five explorers advanced into the cave.

they could hear their own breathing and the steady beating of their hearts. They found themselves straining their eyes to see something—anything—the slightest sign of light, but they could not even tell the difference between opening their eyes and shutting them.

Irene burst out suddenly, "Put on the lights!"

Danny let out his breath with a *whoosh*. They all snapped on their lamps, and as the welcome light flooded the chamber, he said, "It's—it's like being buried alive."

"Don't let's try that experiment again," Irene said, with a shiver. "I just hope we get out of here before our flashlights give out."

"Yes," said the Professor, "perhaps we'd better start back. There are so many ways out of this cave that it would be hopeless for us to try to guess which one will take us back to the surface. At least, we know the way back, and when we come to the stone bridge we'll just have to figure out a way to get across it. I still think we can manage with our ropes."

"All right," said Dr. Tresselt. "Now, which way did we come?"

"Don't worry about that," Danny grinned. "I remembered to drop the thorium nitrate at the entrance. Just let me unpack the Geiger counter."

He got it out and put the earphones over his ears. In his left hand he carried the box which contained the power source and amplifier, and in his right the tube which looked like a microphone but which was the counter itself.

"Let's see," he mused. "I think it was that one, where that shiny dark patch of stone is."

He went to the opening he had indicated, and held the counter close to the ground, moving it to and fro.

"Yep!" he said. "This is it. I can hear the clicking."

He led the way into the tunnel. But they had not gone twenty yards before they came up against a blank wall, deeply scored as if water had churned round and round against it. At the bottom was a dark hole, much too small for them to get through.

"We certainly didn't come up that hole," the Professor observed.

"I must have made a mistake," Danny said. "I guess I was wrong about the clicks."

They retraced their steps, and after searching about for a little while, Danny stopped at another tunnel. "This is the one," he said. "I remember leaning against the pointed rock. Anyway, I *think* I remember. . . ."

He pressed the switch, and passed the counter

back and forth. Then he took off the earphones and held them out. They could all hear the rapid, tiny clicking of the device.

"That's it for sure," said Joe. "Come on, let's get going. This place is giving me the creeps. I'd rather face the stone bridge and know that I was on my way back up to the surface, for sure."

They entered the second tunnel. But in a very short time, its walls closed in and then it came to an end.

"This isn't the one either," said Dr. Tresselt.

They returned to the main chamber, and stared at each other, somewhat fearfully.

"I don't understand," Irene said. "We all heard the clicking. What was it, if it wasn't the radioactive material Danny dropped?"

"Maybe something's wrong with the Geiger counter," said Joe.

"No, I'm sure there's nothing wrong with it, or it wouldn't make any sound at all," said Danny. "Gosh! Maybe—maybe the whole cave is radioactive? Uranium! That's it! Maybe the place is full of uranium."

Dr. Tresselt shook his head. "I find that difficult to believe," he said. "There have been no traces of pitchblende or any such substance. Of course, there are radioactive substances besides uranium which might activate the counter."

Professor Bullfinch nodded. "It is just possible that the cave is mildly radioactive," he said.

"What'll we do, then?" Joe demanded. "There are lots of tunnels. Even if the next one we try doesn't end in a blank wall, how are we going to tell if it's the right one? We can't just wander around for hours and hours and hours. . . . Or can we?"

Nobody answered him. He looked from one to the other. Then he said, "We're stuck, aren't we? Trapped inside a whole mountain of rock. Locked up—and we can't find the key!"

13
A Disappearance

With his usual composure and cheeriness, the Professor took command. "Let's all go back to the 'Altar' and sit down for a moment," he said.

"Sit down? What good will that do?" Joe asked, glumly.

"It will allow us to calm ourselves," said the Professor. "You can't think clearly if you're worried or upset."

He led them to the platform and they sat down on the steps. The Professor pulled out his old pipe and lit it, and after a puff or two, said, "I'll admit the situation looks bad. But I don't think we need give way to absolute despair. It isn't as if there were an infinite number of ways out of this place. There are no more than a dozen or so, and some of those we can cross off because they're smaller than the way we entered by."

Irene said, "Then all we have to do is try one after the other, and sooner or later we'll hit the right one."

"Sure, that's all," Joe said. "A mere nothing. Suppose it takes two or three days? We could die of hunger or thirst, or our lights could wear out. We wouldn't get far in the dark."

"Exactly!" said Professor Bullfinch. "Joe, you've hit it right on the head."

"Gee, really?" Joe said. "Good for me. What'd I say?"

"We must be careful not to waste our lights. Therefore, I suggest that we use only one at a time and save the others. I don't think we'll be here for days. But the sooner we start off, the better. I'll go first, with one of the big battery lamps. You youngsters follow me, and keep your lights off. Alvin, you bring up the rear."

Dr. Tresselt said nothing. He appeared to be deep in thought.

"Alvin!" repeated Professor Bullfinch. "Did you hear me?"

"Er—yes. Yes, yes, yes. Splendid idea. I'm all for it," said Dr. Tresselt, with a start.

The Professor got up, and went up the steps

to stand beside the three big stalactites hanging above the "Altar." "Now, then, let me think a moment," he said. "As I recall it, when we walked up to this stone platform, we saw the three stalactites lined up, one behind the other. If I'm right, the tunnel we want should lie either in *that* direction, or directly opposite."

He pointed, and then climbed down and walked resolutely forward. The beam of his lantern picked out a dark opening between two long ribs of fluted stone. On either side of it other, smaller, holes appeared, but the one in the center seemed to be about the right size.

"It doesn't look *absolutely* familiar," said the Professor, "but let's chance it. Don't forget, even if it isn't the way by which we came, there's always the possibility that it may be another way out to the surface."

He strode forward. The passage, at first just large enough to permit him to walk upright, widened and grew larger. The Professor moved steadily onward. But suddenly, his light shone out into empty space. The floor of the passage ended, and he found that he was standing on the lip of a sheer drop, a kind of miniature cliff, overlooking another large cavern.

"Trouble again," said Joe.

Danny got down on his hands and knees and peered over the brink. "Shine your light down,

Professor Bullfinch," he said. "Look, there's a crack running at a slant down the face of this cliff. It's wide enough to stand on and get your toes into. It goes down—oh, maybe for twenty feet or so, and then I can see gravel, a big bank of it, fanning down in a slope. It wouldn't be hard to get to the bottom."

"Yeah, but what for?" Joe asked. "What's down there?"

"I don't know what's down there, Joe," said the Professor, "but there's something up *here*." He raised one hand, turning it about. "There's a definite current of air here. I can feel it. That may mean an opening—air blowing in from outside."

"Then let's investigate it," said Danny, eagerly.

"I mean to," the Professor replied. "I'll go down first."

"Oh," said Danny.

The Professor took Danny's rope and tied it firmly to a short but thick stalagmite a little way back from the edge. He let it dangle over the drop and followed it down with the beam of his lamp.

"Plenty of line," he said. "You're right, Dan. I don't think it's more than twenty feet to that gravel, and from there I should have no difficulty."

He sat on the edge and put his toes into the shelving crack. "We can break our rule for this once, and use all the lights," he said. "I'll hold the rope as I go. If, when I get to the bottom, it looks promising, I'll call and you can let down the packs and the C-ray, and then come down yourselves. Otherwise, I'll simply climb back."

He winked. "Keep your chins up," he smiled, and started down.

Danny watched from above, holding the beam of his flashlight steady on the Professor's bald head. They saw him reach the gravel and, still holding the rope, make his way downward, sliding and staggering. They could hear the rattle of stones. Then the rope went slack, and they guessed he had come to the end of it and let it go. They saw his light flashing from side to side, and suddenly it vanished.

Before they could speak, it went on again. It shone steadily in one place for a few minutes, and then it began jerking and bobbing in a curious fashion. They heard the Professor call out. Both the distance and the echoes made it impossible to hear what he was saying.

"But that doesn't matter," Danny said. "He told us he'd yell if it was safe. Come on, let's send down the knapsacks."

They hauled up the rope and quickly tied

their packs and the C-ray to it. Slowly and carefully, they let their burden down until they could see it land on the top of the gravel slide.

They waited for the Professor to come up and untie it. But his light remained where it was, and once again they heard him shout something they couldn't understand.

"I'm going down," Danny said, abruptly.

"Oh, Dan, do you think you should?" said Irene, gripping his arm.

"There's something wrong. I've got to go."

He swung himself over the edge and without bothering about the rope edged quickly along the crack, clinging to the rock face with his fingers. It was rough enough to offer him plenty of handholds. He reached the gravel without trouble, and started down it toward the Professor's light, which he could see near the bottom.

"Professor Bullfinch!" he called.

"I'm here," came the answer. "But be careful. Try not to start any of the stones rolling if you can help it."

Picking his way downward, Danny found the Professor seated on a round, smooth boulder with his lamp at his feet. He had one shoe off, and was binding up his ankle with a blood-stained handkerchief.

"I'm afraid it's sprained," he said, apologetically.

Danny fell on his knees. "Let me look," he said.

There was a long, but fortunately rather shallow cut on the Professor's leg. His ankle was bruised and already quite swollen.

"The gravel began slipping under me," the Professor explained. "I lost my balance, and then I caught my foot between two large stones."

"Can you walk?" Danny asked.

"Not very well, I'm afraid. The worst of it is, I'm sure I can't climb back up that cliff."

Danny went to the top of the gravel pile and called to the others. "Come on down."

"What's the matter?" Irene shouted.

"It's the Professor. He's hurt."

As they started down the cliff, Danny untied the C-ray and the knapsacks and carried them to where the Professor sat. He began rummaging in Irene's pack for the first-aid kit. "Be careful," he called, as Irene and Joe came down the slope. "We don't want any more sprained ankles."

Irene, who was an expert in first aid, set to work at once washing the Professor's wound with the rest of the water from the canteen. She

"This could mean trouble."

dressed the sides of the cut with Mercuro-chrome, and then taped up his ankle. "How's that?" she said.

"It feels better already," said the Professor.

Joe, watching with his hands shoved deep in his pockets, said, "You know, this could mean trouble. How are we going to get him back up that cliff?"

The Professor glanced up mildly. "There's one other small point which could mean trouble," he said.

"What?" said Danny, who held the light for Irene, as she repacked her kit.

"Well . . . where, exactly, is Dr. Tresselt?"

The three young people exchanged startled and horrified glances.

"Great jumping gleepers!" said Danny, at last. "I—I forgot all about him. I guess I thought he was following us."

"So did I," said Irene. "And it was dark, too. . . . Now that you mention it, I don't know *when* I last saw him."

They stared at each other, and Joe let out a long groan of despair.

14
A Charm for Engineering

"Well!" said Professor Bullfinch. "This is a fine mess."

"It's a mess all right," Joe said, rolling up his eyes. "But what's fine about it?"

"Maybe he's back in the tunnel a little way," Danny suggested. "He might have stopped to look at something. Let's yell for him."

All together, they shouted at the tops of their voices: "*Doctor Tresselt!* DOCTOR TRESSELT!"

There was no reply.

The young people sank to the ground, and even Professor Bullfinch looked a little discouraged. "I should have thought of this," he said. "It would have been wiser, perhaps, to send him in the lead where we could keep an eye on him."

"But where could he be, Professor?" Irene said.

"I should guess," the Professor answered, "that he saw something which caught his attention back in the glittering cavern, and that he is either still there, or has taken one of the other tunnels. There's no way of telling. When Alvin becomes absorbed in his work he forgets everything else, as you know."

He drew out his faithful pipe and began slowly filling it. "Maybe this will help me think," he said. "Cheer up, friends. We're not finished yet. Don't look so downhearted, Danny. You should know that to a scientist every problem has a solution. It's just a matter of time before we find the answer to this one."

"I wasn't looking sad because of that," Danny said. "I was just thinking—well—that this whole thing is my fault."

"Really? That's very interesting. How do you make that out?"

"I found the cave, didn't I? And I was the one who suggested that we make the trip. And if I had only thought of a simpler way of marking the trail instead of trying to be so scientific—! How was I to know that the whole cavern would be radioactive? And I shouldn't have crossed that stone bridge, either. We might still be safe on the other side.''

The Professor drew at his pipe with enjoyment, and puffed out half a dozen smoke rings. He watched them drift up a little way and then dissolve. ''Dear me,'' he said, ''you have certainly made out a dismal case against yourself. However, Dr. Tresselt was as eager to go as you were, and it was I who agreed to the expedition. I'm afraid your mother was right about us after all. I've hurt my ankle, and Dr. Tresselt is—well—heaven knows where.

''As for the stone bridge, you certainly didn't make it collapse. Alvin and I should have known better than to go across it together. It was our combined weight that made it fall; we were so deep in our discussion that we weren't thinking.

''It's true, the Geiger counter was your idea. Actually, not a bad one, either. As you say, how were you to guess that something would go wrong?''

He grinned at Danny, his eyes twinkling behind his glasses. ''My dear boy, there's no doubt you are headstrong, and you often act without thinking of the consequences. But you mustn't try to take too much blame. Leave some of it for other people!''

He tamped the tobacco down into his pipe with a calloused thumb. "There's a good basic principle I always follow," he went on. "When you can't think of anything to do, just relax. I propose we do just that. I'll rest my ankle so that perhaps I can walk on it a bit, and if we just sit here for a while Alvin may find us of his own accord."

"That's true," Irene said. "He may be in the glittering cave, and when he realizes he's alone he'll follow us."

Joe pulled out his notebook and began scribbling. Danny sat down next to the C-ray and gazed at it mournfully, running his finger along its smooth metal case.

Irene said, "Professor Bullfinch is right, Dan. Stop brooding! I don't blame you, and neither do the others."

"No . . . it isn't that," he replied, with a sigh. "I'm all mixed up, inside. I keep thinking about so many different ideas—getting out of here, and finding Dr. Tresselt, and the Professor's ankle—"

He frowned. "There's something else, too. I keep having the feeling that there's something in the back of my mind, something I've forgotten. If I could only remember what it is, I think we'd know what to do. Something important, too. . . ."

"Well, I hope you remember it," Irene said. She got up and wandered aside a little way, flashing her light on the ground.

Joe cleared his throat. "I don't suppose you'd like to hear a poem I just wrote, would you?"

"A good idea, Joe," said the Professor. "It will make us all feel better, I'm sure. Go ahead."

Joe stuck his pencil behind his ear, and began to read:

"A cave man sat in his cave of stone,
Picking his teeth with an old steak bone.
He felt very brave
While in his cave,
Though he didn't have lights or a telephone.

But all at once he heard a roar,
And a sabertooth tiger was at his door!
The poor old mole
Was in a hole,
And the tiger would have his hide, he swore.

But just as the tiger wrinkled his snout,
The cave man jumped to his feet with a shout.
He grabbed the back wall
And gave it a haul,
And turned his cave right inside out!

Then he was out, and the tiger in,
So he rolled up a rock with a cheerful grin;
He blocked the way
For a week and a day,
And now he's wearing a tiger skin.''

He bowed modestly as the others clapped their hands. ''That's marvelous, Joe,'' Irene exclaimed. ''How do you do it?''

''Oh, I don't know.'' Joe shrugged. ''I just put the pencil on the paper, cross my eyes, and out comes a poem. As far as that goes, I've always wondered how you and Danny manage so easily with arithmetic. That's my worst subject.''

''Well, I'm delighted we have you with us, Joe,'' chuckled the Professor. ''Poetry and science go very well together.''

Danny bent over the C-ray once again. ''If only we could get this thing working,'' he muttered, shining the flashlight on the machine.

''What good would that do?'' said Joe. ''Do you think Dr. Tresselt has turned into a fossil?''

''I can't understand—'' the Professor began.

Danny interrupted him with a yelp. ''Professor Bullfinch! I think I know what's wrong.''

"Really? What is it?" asked the Professor, eagerly.

"It's the knob that controls the focus," said Danny. "Look, when you turn it, it just moves loosely. See? It was held on by a little nut, or something like that, and the nut is gone."

The Professor, supporting himself carefully to keep his weight off his ankle, bent forward to peer at the machine. "Yes, by George! You're right. You have good eyes, my boy. It must have fallen off when we took that slide into the mud."

"Isn't there any way of fixing it?" asked Irene.

"I don't see how," said the Professor. "I didn't bring any spare parts. Unless—perhaps one of the boys has a replacement in his pocket?"

Danny and Joe at once turned their pockets inside out. "We've got enough to stock a general store," Danny sighed. "Rubber bands, pencils, string, paper, stamps, knives, a watch spring, a cog-wheel—you name it. But no nuts or bolts. Isn't that always the way when you want something?"

"Maybe we could hold it on with chewing gum?" Joe suggested.

"A great idea. Got any gum?"

"Um . . . no."

Danny sank back and put his chin in his hands, plunged even deeper into gloom. The Professor turned his pipe over and over as if it might give him an idea. Joe began writing in his notebook, once again, and Irene returned to her searching about on the ground.

Suddenly, she bent and picked something up. "Ah!" she cried. "Maybe this would do."

"What would do what?" asked Danny. "What have you been looking for?"

"You remember, I said I wanted to get something to represent geology on my charm bracelet," Irene said. "I've been keeping my eyes open for some sort of pretty little pebble. I thought that here, where all this gravel has piled up, I might find something. And look— this one is just the right size."

She held out a small, pure white stone, polished and shining, and about the size of her littlest finger nail.

"Maybe my father can drill a hole through it so I can hang it on my bracelet," she said.

Danny had been staring at her in fascination. "Bracelet!" he said.

They all looked at him. "Are you wearing your bracelet?" he went on, in a tense voice.

"Why, of course. Don't you remember?" Irene shook her hand so that the charms jingled together.

"Come here. Let me see it."

So excited was his tone that Irene came to him without another word and held out her wrist.

"Engineering!" Danny said. "I thought so."

"Engi—?" Irene began.

"A small nut and bolt," Danny interrupted. "That's what you used to represent engineering. Just what we need to fix the C-ray. The only question is, is the nut the right size? Take it off the bracelet, Irene."

She did so, and Danny bent over the machine with it while the others turned their lights on him, and watched. He twisted the nut on the threaded rod with fingers that trembled slightly.

"I can just—force it—on," he panted. "I think that will hold it, though."

He straightened up. "Can I try the machine, now, Professor?"

"Why, of course, Dan," said Professor Bullfinch. "I hope it will work, but I don't exactly see how this makes any difference to us."

"It does, though!" Danny snapped the switch, and as the screen grew bright, looked up toward the dark entrance through which they had come, high above them. "This may help us locate Dr. Tresselt."

He frowned. "Let's just try it on that far wall," he said, "and see whether it's working."

He pointed the nozzle of the C-ray at the wall and began turning the knob which regulated the distance of the ray and brought objects into focus. A web of shadows grew on the screen. Slowly, their outlines became clearer, sharpened into long streaks, and then at one corner of the screen they saw a small object come into focus. It looked something like a scallop shell: they could see faint, fluted markings like outspread wings on each side of a central ridge.

"A brachiopod," exclaimed the Professor. "Clearly, a primitive brachiopod."

"Golly!" said Joe. "Is that good?"

"What is it, Professor?" Irene said.

"A shellfish. Something like a—well—like a kind of clam."

"You mean somebody ate clams inside that wall?" said Joe. "How'd he get in there?"

"That shellfish, Joe, may have lived a hundred million years ago," said the Professor, solemnly.

The young people were stunned. "A hundred million—" Irene gasped.

Danny began turning the scanning knob. The shellfish vanished and the streaks began to move sideways, as the ray swept across the wall of stone.

Suddenly Irene cried, ''Stop!''

A set of slightly curved bars came into view.

On the other side of them could be seen the distant silhouette of a man, bent over and tapping at something with a shadowy hammer.

''The clam digger!'' Joe gurgled.

"No, it's not," said Danny. "It's—it's Dr. Tresselt!"

"But look," Irene said, in a hushed voice. "He's in a cage!"

15
The Creature
in the Rocks

Joe's active imagination went right to work.
"Prison!" he said, his eyes wide. "There must
be a race of underground people—like the
Morlocks in *The Time Machine*—people who
have never seen the sun. They must have
sneaked up on him and captured him, and now
he's languishing in one of their dungeons."

Danny cocked his head, eyeing the screen
of the C-ray. "Looks more to me as if he's just
calmly collecting rock samples," he said.

"He's trying to chop his way out," Joe per-
sisted.

"It's a great hypothesis, Joe," said the Professor, "but I think Danny's more likely to be
right. What we take for bars are just some kind

of rock formation—perhaps stalagmites of a slightly different composition than the others.''

Danny had been studying the machine. ''Well, now we know where he is,'' he said. ''The depth setting is on fifty feet. It's about thirty feet from here to the wall of the cave. So he's another twenty feet beyond. I'll bet it's just the next tunnel.'' He jumped up. ''I'm going to see.''

The Professor raised a hand and said, ''Now, don't go charging off in all directions at once.''

''I won't,'' Danny laughed. ''Anyway, this is easy. All I have to do is follow the passage back to the glittering cavern, and then take the next tunnel to the right as I come out. He should be about the same distance down that one. Joe can come with me to see that I don't get into trouble.''

''That's a good idea,'' Joe said. ''But who's going to keep me from getting into trouble?''

''If you boys promise to be very careful, you may go,'' said the Professor. ''But don't go chasing off on your own explorations. Don't take any branch tunnels. For goodness' sake, don't you go getting lost.''

''We'll be careful,'' said Danny. ''Come on, Joe.''

Together, they climbed the gravel slope. The rope was still hanging where they had left it, and they had no trouble getting back to the top of the little cliff. They plunged into the tunnel, Danny in front with the flashlight, and went as quickly as they could until they came out once more in the big cavern with its "Altar" and its sparkling walls. Danny at once turned to his right. There, between two thick folds of rippled green stone was one of the smaller openings they had noticed before.

"Too bad you can't see footprints in the rock," said Joe.

"Yes, but I'll bet anything this is the way he went," Danny answered.

They entered, stooping. The floor of this passage was uneven and jagged, and it sloped steeply downward. It was, in fact, more like a deep fissure than a tunnel, as if an earthquake had moved and split the rock and opened a narrow way down to the depths.

"How far shall we go?" Joe asked. "Maybe this isn't the way at all. How are we going to tell?"

"Hard to say." Danny climbed over a sharp knife-edge, holding the light above his head to keep it from banging against the stone. "Can't judge distance in this one because it isn't flat, like the other. Let's go on for a while, and then worry about it if nothing turns up."

But as it happened, they didn't have too far

to go. A few moments later, Joe, who had paused to wait for Danny to climb down out of his way, spotted a yellow glow on the walls ahead. An instant later, they could both hear, quite clearly, the clink and tap of a hammer.

They slid down a last sloping slab and found themselves in a chamber whose dull gray and brown walls were in sharp contrast to the big cavern they had just left. Dr. Tresselt was on his knees examining some bits of stone by the light of his lantern, which stood on a point of rock nearby.

"Dr. Tresselt!" said Danny. "We've found you!"

The geologist glanced at them over his shoulder. "Um?" he said, in an abstracted tone. "Were you lost?"

Danny laughed. "No, sir. But you are."

"I am?" The geologist raised his eyebrows. "I don't feel lost. I know where I am."

Then, slowly, as the meaning of Danny's words penetrated, his expression changed. "Oh, dear," he said. "I am sorry. I assure you, I didn't mean to wander off. But you see, I noticed those same red streaks at the entrance to this passageway, and I just couldn't resist investigating. The further I went, the more clay I found. Look about you—! This chamber is not limestone like the others, but was hollowed out of petrified mud. I have found the fossils of several fresh-water molluscs, too. See?''

He held out what looked like small, dark pebbles.

Danny said, ''But where's the cage?''

''What?'' said Dr. Tresselt. ''What are you talking about? You're *in* the cave.''

''But where are the bars?''

''Why should there be bars in a cave?''

''Not cave, Dr. Tresselt,'' said Joe. ''Cage. C-a-g-e.''

''Cage? This isn't a cage. Why do you keep calling it one?''

''We saw it on the C-ray screen,'' Danny said. ''Just as plain as could be. Big curving bars, and you were inside them.''

''Well, I'm not,'' Dr. Tresselt said. ''I'm afraid my friend Euclid expects too much from that invention of his. What you saw was probably a defect of some sort—something wrong with the machine.''

''There's nothing wrong with the C-ray,'' said Danny, firmly. ''We saw one of those fossil shellfish you've found, stuck in the stone. But it's certainly very funny that there isn't anything here that would look like bars.'' He flashed his lamp all about the small chamber.

"Anyway, let's join the others. We'll have to decide what to do, now that the Professor has hurt his ankle."

"How did that happen?" asked Dr. Tresselt, gathering up his things.

"He slipped on some gravel and twisted his leg. Maybe you'll have some idea how to get him back up the cliff."

They hurried back up the steep passage and were soon standing once more on the top of the cliff. Dr. Tresselt was agile and used to climbing, and he went down the sheer face like a mountaineer. Joe followed, and then Danny untied the rope and let it fall so that they could use it if necessary.

Professor Bullfinch waved, as they picked their way down the gravelly slope. "We've been expecting you," he said. "We watched you boys find Dr. Tresselt, on the C-ray screen."

"Do you mean to say that that thing works?" Dr. Tresselt said.

"Perfectly. How do you think we found you? We saw you through the wall of the chamber. By the way, what was that rock formation that looks like a cage?"

"A cage? Danny said something about that," said the geologist. "There was no such formation where I was. Let me see that apparatus.''

He squatted down and stared at the screen of the C-ray. He whistled softly between his teeth, and said, ''Is there any way of moving the picture from side to side?''

''Oh, yes. We watched you as you climbed back up the passageway. This is the scanning dial. Turn this button to one side or the other.''

Dr. Tresselt did so. ''What about focus?'' he asked.

Professor Bullfinch showed him what to do. For a few moments he sat absorbed, moving first one knob, then the other. On the screen, a strange shape grew, its outlines clear and dark. It looked like a fan, with a large hole below it like an eye, then a curved eagle's beak, and two spiky horns jutting forward.

''Congratulations, Euclid!'' Dr. Tresselt said, in a voice that trembled with excitement. ''Your C-ray is more than a success. Look at that! Doesn't it look familiar?''

The Professor stared. Then, almost in a whisper, he said, ''It does indeed. A fossil skull. The skull of a dinosaur!''

16
"Light Your Pipe!"

The Professor put a finger on the fanlike shape showing on the screen. "One of the Ceratopsia," he said. "And from the three horns, I would say it was *Triceratops*."

"My feeling, too," agreed Dr. Tresselt.

"And what we thought were the bars of a cage—"

"Were its ribs, somewhat out of focus!"

"A tri—sephera—what you said," Joe put in. "You mean, one of those giant prehistoric lizards?"

"The fossil skeleton of one, Joe," said Dr. Tresselt. "And a fine specimen, too, I should judge, although I can't make out all the details from this shadow picture. You can see the long horns and sharp beak, and the big bony shield that swept up behind the head to protect the neck. Watch, now, as I move the ray. You can see the ribs, and there's part of the backbone and the long heavy tail."

"If it wasn't in the cave with you," said the Professor, "where was it?"

"I think I can answer that," Dr. Tresselt said. "It's embedded in the wall between this cave and that one."

"In the solid limestone?" said the Professor. "Isn't that a little unusual?"

"It would be exceedingly unusual, if the wall were really limestone," said Dr. Tresselt. "But I'll explain all that later. Meanwhile, we've got the problem of what to do with you. Can you walk at all?"

Professor Bullfinch got carefully to his feet and took a step or two. He winced. "It's pretty tender," he said. "However, I think I can hobble along on it."

"Hobbling won't get us very far, not along these underground ways," said Dr. Tresselt, thoughtfully. "If the ground were fairly level it wouldn't be so bad, but I don't quite see how you're going to get over that fallen stone slab, for instance."

"Maybe we could make a stretcher out of a jacket and two long poles," said Irene.

"That's one of the things they taught us in my first-aid class."

"Poles? Where would we get them, in these caves?" Dr. Tresselt asked.

"Maybe we could use long, thin stalactites," Danny suggested.

The Professor shook his head. "I think you'd find them harder to break off than you imagine," he said. "In any case, I doubt that you could carry me all the way back. No, Alvin, I'm afraid we've got to face it. You will have to leave me here."

Dr. Tresselt pursed up his lips in a soundless whistle. Then he said, "Wouldn't think of it."

"But you must. You can all go back and when you're out you can send help back for me. As long as I have my pipe and tobacco and some matches, and one of the flashlights, I'll be all right."

"Well, I won't leave you, Professor," said Irene. "I'll stay here and keep you company. Let the boys go back."

"Alone? I don't like that idea," the Professor said.

"And I don't want to leave you here, either," said Danny.

"Well, we can't send Dr. Tresselt back by himself," said Dr. Tresselt, with a grin. "I might find something interesting along the

way, and get side-tracked, and forget where I was supposed to be going."

The Professor sighed. "We're not getting anywhere with this discussion," he said. "Somebody has got to go. What else can we do?"

"We could try hoddering for hep," Joe said, thickly. "Or sed up smoke sigdals." He sneezed loudly, and, taking out his handkerchief, blew his nose like a trumpet.

The Professor couldn't help laughing. "Smoke signals," he said. "A very good idea,

Joe. Or we might try sending a telegram: *Trapped in cave send help love to all.* I'm afraid that wouldn't work, either.''

Danny clapped his hands together, so sharply and suddenly that they all jumped and turned to look at him.

"Wait a minute!" he cried. "That's it!"

"Whad's id?" said Joe.

"You!" Danny exclaimed.

Joe stepped back a pace. "Now, waid a middud—"

"Your nose," Danny went on, excitedly. "And smoke signals. I've got it! That's what I've been trying to remember ever since we got stuck down here."

Dr. Tresselt looked completely baffled. "Nose?" he mumbled. "Smoke signals? I'm afraid this is too deep for me."

"Danny," said the Professor, "pull yourself together. Tell us what you mean."

Danny had been capering about madly. Now he stopped. "Your pipe!" he said. "Professor —light your pipe!"

17
Into the Open

The Professor gave a long sigh. "My poor boy," he said. "Just sit down for a minute and rest, and try to relax."

"See if there's any water left in the canteen," said Dr. Tresselt, in a worried tone. "Maybe a cold compress on his forehead—"

Danny laughed merrily. "Don't worry," he said, "I haven't gone crazy. I told you there was something I was trying to remember. Well, when we first stood up there on the top of the cliff and looked down into this chamber, Professor Bullfinch said there was a current of air blowing through. But we had so many other things to think about that we forgot it. Later, when he lit his pipe and started blowing smoke rings, they floated up perfectly a little way and then dissolved. If we'd thought about it, then, we'd have seen where the breeze was coming from."

"Of course!" said Dr. Tresselt.

"And then Joe sneezed," Danny continued. "Look at him. His eyes are watering and his nose is all red. Irene, you know what that means."

"His allergy!" said Irene. "He's allergic to goldenrod."

"But there's no goldenrod down here," the Professor objected.

"No, but there's lots of it on Rose Hill, and the far side of Sugarloaf is covered with it," said Danny. "Do you know what I think? I think we've traveled right through Sugarloaf, under the ground, and now we're near the surface on the side facing Rose Hill. The air is blowing in here from some hole leading to the outside, and it's carrying goldenrod pollen. It can't be too far from the outside, or I'd guess there wouldn't be enough pollen to start Joe's allergy working. Right?"

"By George, I believe the boy has something," said Dr. Tresselt.

"He has the makings of a scientist," said Professor Bullfinch, proudly. "Hold on, now, while I light my pipe. Then we can trace the course of the air current by watching the smoke.''

In a short time, he had his pipe going. Dr. Tresselt focused the beam of one of the battery lamps on the plume of blue smoke. Deliberately, the Professor puffed away and sent three round, fat smoke rings floating lazily above his head. They wavered, and shredded away.

''That way!'' Danny pointed to the wall of the cave opposite the side down which they had climbed. ''Dr. Tresselt, you help the Professor. Professor, keep blowing smoke and walk toward that wall. Come on, Joe and Irene, bring the other lights and let's see what we can find.''

The wall at which he had pointed rose in a gradual slope above their heads. At the bottom, it consisted of boulders and large chunks of broken stone. But when they had climbed over these, Danny, standing on a flat outcrop, gave a yell.

''There's earth here!'' he cried. ''In among the stones, there's plain old dirt.''

Irene clambered a little higher and flashed her light at the Professor's smoke cloud. ''I think the air is blowing from up here,'' she said. ''Yes—I can feel it on my face. Warm air, a steady stream of it.''

Danny joined her, and together they crawled

up still further until they were near the rocky roof of the cave.

"Turn off your light," Danny said to Irene. And when she had done so, he tapped her arm and said, "Now look over there, to your left, where that big chunk of rock is."

She blinked. A faint pencil of yellow light shone through a crack in the earth.

"It's sunlight," said Danny, with satisfaction.

He scrambled over to the crack and began to dig recklessly, throwing out the dirt with both hands like a puppy.

"Watch out!" squealed Irene. "You're showering me!"

He stopped, but already he had made a hole as big as his head. The others, down below, could see the golden daylight come streaming in.

"This is all loose dirt," Danny said. "It seems to be held in place by a few big slabs of stone. If Joe comes up here and helps me, we can really excavate."

In a very short time, the two boys had grubbed away an opening large enough for Danny to squeeze through. He went out, head-first. An instant later, he grinned down at them and waved.

"I've got a pointed stick," he said. "Watch

out, Joe. Now you're going to see the dirt fly."

He attacked the edges of the hole, and with Joe helping as best he could from the inside, they soon made it large enough so that the men could get out.

"Professor Bullfinch," Danny called. "Do you think you can crawl up the slope with the rope to help you?"

"My trousers may suffer," the Professor answered, "but I think I can manage."

Irene brought the rope up and climbed out of the hole. She and Danny held it fast, while Dr. Tresselt and Joe helped the Professor up over the rocks at the bottom. Then, holding the rope to steady himself, the Professor slowly and laboriously made his way up to the edge of the hole, and so out into the sunlight.

The others followed, bringing the C-ray and the knapsacks. They stood on the hillside, blinking, and Joe spoke for all of them when he said, "It feels as if we'd been let out of school half a day early!"

They had emerged on a shoulder of the mountain just above a long, narrow valley which separated it from Rose Hill, which was somewhat lower and more rounded than Sugarloaf. They sat down to catch their breaths, and to bask for a while in the warmth of the sun after their hours in the cool, dank darkness.

18
Radioactive Danny

Danny said, "I'm just wondering—can't we go back later and try to dig out the skeleton of the dinosaur?"

Dr. Tresselt chuckled. "I'm afraid that job's a little beyond our skill, Dan. Dinosaur fossils are easily broken, and in the case of a good one, such as this seems to be, it will take a whole gang of men to get it out properly. I'll have to notify my friend Dr. Purdy, at the Natural History Museum."

"What will he do?"

"Well, he'll bring down a crew and first they'll cut away all the rock above the skeleton so that they can get down to it. Then, they'll start chiseling out the rock around it, painting the bones as they expose them with shellac to preserve them. With a specimen of this size they will probably then cut it up into blocks so that they can handle it easily. Each block will be coated with burlap covered with plaster, and marked for identification. When the plaster is hard, the blocks will be shipped off to the museum, where the staff will go to work on them. They'll spend weeks cleaning, preparing, and studying the fossil.''

He looked about him. ''Are you sure you can find this place again, Dan?''

''Oh, yes. But to be on the safe side, I'll mark it.'' Danny took up the long, pointed stick which he had used for digging, and thrust it into the ground a little way above the hole.

''Good. I should think that the museum would be very grateful to you youngsters,'' said Dr. Tresselt. ''It isn't every day a fine specimen like this comes along, and you all helped find it. You'll be able to feel rather proud of yourselves, when you see your names on the card the museum displays with this dinosaur.''

''The thing I don't understand,'' said Danny, ''is how the dinosaur got down there and was buried inside the rock. Do you think there was an earthquake, and the tri—tricycle—whatever it was—was caught in it?''

"*Triceratops,*" said Dr. Tresselt. "The name means 'three-horned face.' It had three horns, one above each eye and the third on the beak, something like the horn of a rhinoceros. *Triceratops* was a plant-eating dinosaur. It lived at about the same time as *Tyrannosaurus,* the 'tyrant lizard,' a huge meat-eater which ran on two legs, had a mouth full of teeth as long as your arm, weighed six or seven tons, and could look over the roof of your house. In spite of all this, it had a hard time making its dinner off *Triceratops* because the plant-eater's neck was protected by a large fan, or collar, of bone, and the three horns and sharp beak made it a hard nut to crack.

"Your question about how it was buried is a good one. I don't know the answer, of course, but I can make a guess which *may* be something like what really happened."

He stood up, shading his eyes, and waved his arm. "Perhaps Professor Bullfinch has told you that we believe this whole region was once covered by a sea," he said. "These limestone hills are made of sediment—minerals, shells— that settled slowly to the bottom of that sea in the course of millions of years. Then the sea dried up, or drew away, and the earth changed. Where the sea had been, there were rivers

which washed dirt and mud and clay down into
the valleys.

"This valley, between these hills, may once
have held such a river. For many reasons, it,
too, began to dry up and grow shallow. Perhaps
there were marshes here, with a muddy bottom.

"One day, *Triceratops* may have been
browsing in the reeds or grasses. Perhaps the
big tyrant lizard chased him; perhaps he stum-
bled into quicksand and couldn't escape. He
sank down into the mud—he was very heavy,
after all—and was buried.

"And more centuries passed, thousands of
years, millions—more than a hundred million
years. Imagine it! In all that time, the ground
sank and rose many times, very slowly, and
the mud turned to stone, and the skeleton of
Triceratops, snugly encased in it, turned to a
kind of stone as well. That petrified mud was
the wall of the cave down below, not limestone
at all, but the ancient marsh. There the fossil
lay, waiting for us to find it, an animal that
lived and died long before even the first tiny
ancestor of man appeared on the earth."

He fell silent, and the young people sat with
their chins on their knees, trying to imagine
that distant past.

Professor Bullfinch nodded, and said, "Help

me up, Alvin. I think it's time we went home. Mrs. Dunn will be wondering what has become of us."

They put on their packs and Danny found another stick to serve as a cane for the Professor.

Irene, looking back at the hole through which they had crawled, said, "There's one thing. . . . When they get through cutting away the rock around that *Triceratops*, we'll have a new, big entrance to the caves. People will be able to explore them, to go right through the mountain."

Joe covered his eyes with his hands. "I can see it in my mind," he said. "Guided tours— electric lights—souvenirs—me with a beautiful guide's uniform leading the people around— No! Wait a minute, change that. I'll be sitting out here taking tickets, and you kids can be leading the people around."

"Leading people—!" Danny snapped his fingers. "Nothing doing. We've got to keep everybody away for a while."

"What do you mean, Dan? Why?" asked Irene. "It isn't that dangerous. Anyway, we can put a bridge over that gap, and mark the passageways, and—"

"I wasn't thinking of danger," Danny replied. "I was thinking of our making a fortune from our mine."

They all gaped at him with their mouths open. "Our *mine?* What mine?" asked the Professor, at last.

"Our uranium mine! My gosh, have you all forgotten how we were stuck in the glittering cavern? How the Geiger counter blipped wherever I turned it? The place must be loaded with radioactive ore. I'll bet this whole hillside is radioactive."

He slipped off his pack and quickly took out the Geiger counter. "Just wait a sec," he said. "It won't take long. Let me make a check on it."

He put on the earphones and pressed the switch, turning the counter toward the ground. "It is!" he exclaimed. "It's clicking like anything!"

He began to scout about, first up the hill slope, then down. His eyes were dancing, and his face was split by an immense grin. "It's all radioactive, wherever I turn the thing," he said. "We'll be rich. We'll have the biggest mine in America."

The Professor had been watching him with puckered brows. He said, "Danny, I find this difficult to believe. The whole hillside—?"

"Try it for yourself," Danny said. He took

off the earphones and handed the instrument to the Professor. Professor Bullfinch slipped the phones on and pressed the switch. They watched him eagerly.

"Nothing," he said.

"Nothing?" Danny goggled at him. "But—but I *heard* it—"

"You try it, Alvin." The Professor handed the Geiger counter to the geologist.

Dr. Tresselt began moving about slowly, pointing the counter this way and that a little distance above the surface of the earth. "Not a sound," he said. "Very curious. Unless—"

"Unless what?" asked the Professor.

"Unless *Danny* is radioactive."

With that, he turned the counter toward Danny's feet.

"Aha!" he cried. "Listen to this." He held up the earphones, and they could all hear the faint ticks.

Danny turned pale. Then, his face grew very red. Without a word, he bent down and turned the cuff of his trouser leg inside out. Some small white crystals, well mixed with fluff and dust, fell out.

The Professor raised his eyebrows. "Thorium nitrate?"

Danny nodded sheepishly. "When I dropped it to mark the place where the passageway di-

"It's all radioactive."

vided, some must have fallen into the cuff of my pants."

He smiled ruefully at his friends. "Well, there goes a fortune," he said.

Dr. Tresselt's brown, seamed face wrinkled

with amusement. "I think, " he said, "that we've already found something even better than a fortune. Everything that science can find out about this earth we live on is valuable and important. The caves, the fossil of *Triceratops,* will help us learn a bit more about the history of our planet, will tell us a few more of its secrets, and perhaps even help us to make some good guesses about its future."

"I know," said Danny, smiling up into the faces of the two scientists.

"Sure, I agree," said Joe. "But golly, you can't buy ice-cream sodas with just knowledge."

"Oh, if that's the problem, I think we can solve it easily," said Professor Bullfinch. "Just help me limp down to the house and get settled comfortably, and then I think you can make the soda fountain with ample time to spare before dinner."

He took up his stick and put his free hand on Dan's shoulder, for support. Then, slowly, but joyfully, the Bullfinch-Tresselt Undergound Expedition marched down the hill to Midston and its reward.

Authors' Note

Much of the cave material described in this book is drawn from actual exploration of caves, made over a number of years with my son, Christopher, a member of the National Speleological Society. For readers who would like to try underground adventures for themselves, a list of some caves open to the public follows. These are all safe to enter and have guided tours, but it should be remembered that caving can be extremely dangerous, and that no beginner should try exploring new or unknown caves without plenty of experienced supervision.

Crystal Caverns, Trussville, Alabama
Colossal Cave, Vail, Arizona
Diamond Caverns, Jasper, Arkansas
Boyden Cave, Sequoia National Forest, California
Cave of the Winds, Manitou Springs, Colorado
Florida Caverns, Florida Caverns State Park, near
  Marianna, Florida
Cave Springs Cave, Cedartown, Georgia
Craters of the Moon Caves, near Arco, Idaho
Burksville Cave, Burksville, Illinois
Donaldson Cave, Spring Mill State Park, Mitchell,
  Indiana
Crystal Lake Cave, near Dubuque, Iowa
Mammoth Cave, Mammoth Cave National Park,
  Kentucky
Anemone Cave, Acadia National Park, Bar Harbor,
  Maine
Crystal Grottoes, Boonsboro, Maryland
Mystery Cave, Spring Valley, Minnesota
Bridal Cave, Camdenton, Missouri
Lewis and Clark Cavern, Lewis and Clark Cavern State
  Park, Whitehall, Montana
Lehman Caves, Baker, Nevada
Lost River Caverns, North Woodstock, New Hampshire
Carlsbad Caverns, Carlsbad Caverns National Park,
  Carlsbad, New Mexico
Howe Caverns, Cobbleskill, New York
Linville Caverns, Ashford, North Carolina
Seneca Caverns, Bellevue, Ohio
Alabaster Caverns, Freedom, Oklahoma
Oregon Caves National Monument, Crater Lake
  National Park, Oregon

Indian Caverns, Spruce Creek, Pennsylvania
Jewel Cave, Wind Cave National Park, Hot Springs,
   South Dakota
Bristol Caverns, Bristol, Tennessee
Cascade Caverns, Boerne, Texas
Timpanogos Cave, American Fork, Utah
Luray Caverns, Luray, Virginia
Organ Cave, Ronceverte, West Virginia
Chelan Ice Caves, Lake Chelan State Park, Chelan,
   Washington
Crystal Cave, Spring Valley, Wisconsin

This list was drawn from *Exploring American Caves,* by Franklin Folsom, Crown Publishers, Inc., New York, 1962, which not only contains a much more complete and detailed list of caves, but also much exciting information on cave exploration.

ABOUT THE AUTHORS
AND ILLUSTRATOR

JAY WILLIAMS has written over forty-five fiction and nonfiction books for children of all ages, in addition to coauthoring fifteen books about Danny Dunn. Mr. Williams was born in Buffalo, New York, and educated at the University of Pennsylvania, Columbia University, and the Art Students League.

RAYMOND ABRASHKIN wrote and coproduced the very popular and successful "Little Fugitive," a film that won an award at the Venice Film Festival.

BRINTON TURKLE was born in Alliance, Ohio. He studied art at the School of the Boston Museum of Fine Arts and the Institute of Design in Chicago. He has been active in the theater, and has both written and illustrated many books for children, including *The Adventures of Obadiah*.